$EM=C^2$

A New Formula for Enrollment Management

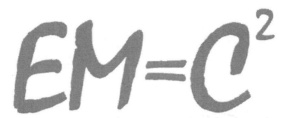

John Maguire
Lawrence Butler
&
Their Colleagues at Maguire Associates

Order this book online at www.trafford.com/08-0731
or email orders@trafford.com

Most Trafford titles are also available at major online book retailers.

Note for Librarians: A cataloguing record for this book is available from Library
and Archives Canada at www.collectionscanada.ca/amicus/index-e.html

Printed in Victoria, BC, Canada.

ISBN: 978-1-4251-6875-9

*We at Trafford believe that it is the responsibility of us all, as both individuals
and corporations, to make choices that are environmentally and socially sound.
You, in turn, are supporting this responsible conduct each time you purchase a
Trafford book, or make use of our publishing services. To find out how you are
helping, please visit www.trafford.com/responsiblepublishing.html*

*Our mission is to efficiently provide the world's finest, most comprehensive
book publishing service, enabling every author to experience success.
To find out how to publish your book, your way, and have it available
worldwide, visit us online at www.trafford.com/10510*

www.trafford.com

North America & international
toll-free: 1 888 232 4444 (USA & Canada)
phone: 250 383 6864 ♦ fax: 250 383 6804
email: info@trafford.com

The United Kingdom & Europe
phone: +44 (0)1865 722 113 ♦ local rate: 0845 230 9601
facsimile: +44 (0)1865 722 868 ♦ email: info.uk@trafford.com

10 9 8 7 6 5 4 3

Contents

Introduction

If you are someone with a stake in the long-term success of a college or university, some of the following vignettes[1] are likely to be painfully familiar.

- **Stealth Applicants**

  Virginia Rhodes, VP of Enrollment Management at Thoreau University, is disturbed to discover that 40 percent of the current year's applicants were unknown to the school prior to sending in their applications. These "stealth applicants" had done all their research online without ever once contacting the school. The percentage of stealth applicants has risen four years in a row. Has this enrollment manager lost control of Thoreau U's recruitment funnel?

- ## What a Wicked Web
  Dr. Benjamin Plutarch, president of Saint Constanza College, is alarmed that a baseless but scandal-creating rumor started by a single prank post on YouTube – and now spreading like wildfire through the blogosphere – has created a public relations nightmare for a school with a deep faith tradition. The local media outlets are calling, and Saint Constanza's biggest alumni fundraiser wants Plutarch to fix the situation *now*. Even worse are the angry e-mails from parents and the withdrawal of acceptances by twelve students, a difficult loss for a small college. How can the president handle this crisis in a way that upholds Constanza's values and limits the enrollment damage?

- ## Seduction Most Rank
  Oldham University sets itself apart from the crowd by providing its students with the opportunity to learn from the highly regarded CEOs, actors, and musicians who serve on its large adjunct faculty. In spite of this, Oldham president Dr. Candace Roberts finds herself preparing to argue at an upcoming board meeting for reducing the percentage of part-time faculty. The university's own research shows that this seductively simple move will significantly improve Oldham's rankings in *US News & World Report*. But will this move mean that the school is abandoning one of the most distinctive and valued features of its educational philosophy—the involvement of real-world practitioners in the training of students?

- ## Underendowed Ambitions
  The Senior VP for Marketing & Communications at West University, a high-quality, second-tier institution, wonders what to do in the wake of President Rich Pockets' recent, high-profile announcements about his impossibly high aspirations for the school. West's senior leaders are not sure how they will find the funds to fulfill all these promises while still increasing affordability and access for students, never mind counter the challenges posed by West's more elite aspirant – and better-endowed

– competitors, which have announced that *they* will reduce their effective tuition costs while improving their offering quality. Can West compete, or should it try to define its own turf?

- ## Global Poaching
  Susan Smith, the Director of Enrollment at Staple University, has realized that a disturbingly high number of prospects from traditional feeder schools have chosen to apply to and attend colleges outside the United States. The school's competition for students who were once its bread-and-butter applicants is no longer limited to other domestic institutions, but increasingly includes schools in Canada, Europe, and Asia. As she prepares her summary of the university's enrollment picture for an Executive Committee meeting, she wonders whether this marks a trend. If it's not a fluke, how should the institution's leaders respond?

As consultants to numerous colleges and universities, we are hearing stories like these with increasing frequency. And each time we hear them, we also hear a challenge to what had been a carefully constructed sense of control, as well as a real anxiety about how to cope with these challenges. In the media, at conference tables and trustee forums, people concerned about their institution's continued ability to shape its future or, even more basically, its student enrollment, are asking some difficult questions:

- When more and more candidates for admission are "stealth applicants" totally unknown to the institution yet who "know" the institution through what they learn on the Internet, what has become of our **control over student recruitment and messaging**?

- When any message posted by anyone can gain traction through an ever-expanding universe of online social networks, what has become of our **control over institutional reputation**?

- When the power of third party entities like *US News & World Report* to define the metrics by which the relative quality of schools is judged can encourage institutional leaders to game the system at the expense of their own values and long-term competitive best interests, what has become of our **control over institutional distinctiveness and destiny**?

- When the endowment disparity between a handful of elite institutions and the great bulk of highly tuition-dependent schools creates a permanent disadvantage on the part of the latter in terms of programmatic quality and price, what has become of our **control over the competitive dynamics** among institutions?

- When the standing of universities in other countries has so improved in relation to our own in terms of both academics and costs, and when awareness of all this is a mere mouse-click away, what has become of our **control over the national boundaries** that define our student markets?

If there actually ever was any real control by institutional leaders over any of the above, it's gone now. The Internet-Third Party Influencer- Endowment Disparity- Globalization genie is officially out of the bottle. And we'd all better get used to it. Does that mean Enrollment Management (EM) is now an oxymoron? That enrollment cannot be managed?

The answer to that question is No. While the traditional notion of EM is inadequate to cope with the new realities, a thoughtful examination of these EM challenges actually reveals opportunities hidden within – opportunities that can be discerned and exploited by adopting a new way of thinking about Enrollment Management. This new understanding of EM offers real hope for the many colleges and universities seeking to secure for themselves and those they serve a strong, vibrant future.

This book describes a new approach to Enrollment Management. We offer it with the hope of starting a conversation about what happens next.

The Book in Brief

On one level, this book tells a story about the evolution of Enrollment Management, from its origins as a set of ideas just beginning to coalesce in the minds of a group of college admissions managers some 30 years ago right up through today and, we hope, beyond. On another level, though, it's a story about higher education in the United States at the beginning of the twenty-first century and where – for good or ill – it seems to be heading. We make no grand claims of expertise on the latter theme; but as to EM we feel we can speak with some authority. One of us – Jack Maguire – was there at the beginning (and is referred to by many as "the father of Enrollment Management," a paternity he neither promotes nor denies) and both of us earn our living as professional consultants/researchers with well over 50 years between us in serving clients in higher education. More importantly, we are surrounded by a group of colleagues at Maguire Associates who have contributed their insights and perspectives to this book and who, if we must say so ourselves, really do know what they're talking about.

We can confidently say that you, the reader of this book, already know a great deal about Enrollment Management, Higher Education and a whole lot more. So, our goal is neither to cover ground you already know nor to presume to predict the future during this most fluid of times. Rather, we hope to pique your interest just enough to initiate a conversation that will continue long after you've finished reading this slim tome. The web site and the blog already await you (more about that on page 133).

We also know you are busy. So, here's a quick summary of the main points we make in this book.

- Enrollment Management (EM) grew out of a set of ideas and principles that responded to compelling needs affecting colleges and universities some 30 years ago.

- From the start, EM was about creating strategic alignment and coherent messaging across the institution and building a high degree of interpersonal collaboration within and across functions, all guided by strong institutional leadership.

- Over the years, EM has evolved in response to changing realities in the marketplace and forces impinging on higher education. As competition among schools has increased, EM has taken on more and more of the trappings and language of marketing, including the "sales funnel" metaphor and all of the other corporate marketing tools and techniques: market research, modeling, positioning, branding, etc.

- Contributing to this preoccupation with short-term marketing advantage is the inordinate influence of *US News* and other publishers of college rankings – a development that has entangled college presidents, trustees, enrollment officials and other institutional leaders in a serious double bind. Either they subscribe to the mantra of marketing-at-all-costs – even to the extent of gaming the system to optimize the school's ranking – or risk the erosion of institutional reputation and loss of competitive standing.

- As a result, in far too many schools, Enrollment Management has become more about gaining short-term competitive advantage at the point of enrollment and less about finding the best fit between school and student to the long-term benefit of each.

- Not surprisingly, we've witnessed a backlash against EM, which many view as a commercial wolf in nonprofit sheep's clothing that promotes the commoditization of higher education through the deployment of an array of PR tactics.

- We are not advocating that the *position* of Enrollment Management VP necessarily be the senior position to which all others report, but rather that the *discipline* of Enrollment Management be reflected in Marketing and Communications and throughout the enterprise.

- The problem is not with Enrollment Management *per se*, but with the fact that EM as currently practiced has been not only co-opted by the rankings pressure but also has failed to keep pace with other dramatic changes affecting institutions of higher education today —particularly, the dramatic growth of the Internet and the geometrically exploding number of services, relationships, and decision complexities it has spawned.

- Fortunately, this unprecedented explosion of information can be harnessed in the interest of deriving levels of meaning heretofore unimagined. Advances in information technology and the emergence of integrated databases make possible a wealth of new knowledge and insight about the many communities served by the institution.

- Adopting a new, more expansive approach to Enrollment Management is an essential first step in leveraging these new technologies in ways that are more responsive to today's challenges and opportunities.

- The conventional enrollment "funnel" is too Newtonian to adequately describe this new world of multiple, on-line and on-ground communities. Instead, inspired by Einstein's elegant formula, we need to think of EM in terms of the new physics with all of its uncertainty, simultaneity, distributed responsibility, multidimensionality, and "order within chaos."

- We need to expand our thinking to include the cultivating, nurturing, and leveraging of a Community of Communities (C^2) – including communities of influence, as well as communities of students, faculty, alumni, advocates, stewards, donors, etc. $EM=C^2$ is our name for this reformulation of Enrollment Management – a new EM with Community at its core.

- Introducing a C^2 sensibility to the practice of Enrollment Management will require a good deal of structured experimentation and the best thinking of many practitioners, sharing their ideas, successes, and failures in a robust discussion beginning with this book but extending online and over time.

So, after 30 years, we believe Enrollment Management has only begun to fulfill its potential. The times call for replenishing the EM tool box with new tools and, more importantly, with a higher expectation of Enrollment Management as a professional discipline. But first, institutions of higher education must let go of the illusory sense of direct control of an enrollment process that, like it or not, has already slipped away from such control. Only then can they assert a far more effective kind of indirect influence – through data-driven insight, values-based inspiration, highly responsive assistance, and flexible facilitation.

We wrote this book because we care deeply about the importance of higher education in expanding the horizons and lifting the lives of people young and old, and because as professional consultants who are honored to assist those charged with fulfilling this noble purpose, we are concerned about assuring the continued efficacy of a critical administrative function – namely, Enrollment Management.

We believe adopting a C^2 approach can help EM practitioners regain the high ground and a new sense of institutional ownership of the terms shaping the current debate over the metrics, the messages and the methods used in marketing higher education to all of its many student and donor communities.

The Four *Chronicle* Surveys

This book draws upon an array of information sources, including the professional literature, our own several decades' worth of consulting experience, and the collective, eclectic experience of our Maguire Associates colleagues. In addition to that, we felt the subject matter and timing were particularly propitious for sharing some of the more pertinent findings from the four important survey studies that Maguire Associates has conducted over the past few years in partnership with The *Chronicle of Higher Education*:

- In the first study (2005), we surveyed 764 **presidents** of colleges and universities and learned about their experiences and attitudes, as well as how they spend their time.

- In 2006, we surveyed **high school teachers** and **university faculty members** who addressed questions about how well prepared students are for the demands of college-level work.

- The third survey, conducted in 2007, focused on college and university **governing board members** and was perhaps the first large-scale survey to address this hard-to-reach group. We were able to compare the perspectives of board members and presidents on a number of issues.

- Finally, we have recently completed (2008) a survey of 461 senior-level **admissions** and **enrollment management officials**. We learned about their own background, how their offices are organized, some of their policies and practices, and their attitudes about a number of the hot issues of the day.

Findings from these surveys and verbatim comments from the respondents will be presented at appropriate points in the text that follows.

How the Book is Organized

The first three chapters make the case for why a new formulation of Enrollment Management is needed. Chapters 4 through 9 present our thoughts about what we feel that new formulation – $EM=C^2$ – should be. Chapters 10 through 14 revisit the five "challenging opportunities" that introduce this book and show how they can be addressed using the $EM=C^2$ model. We conclude in Chapter 15 with a brief discussion of the implementation challenges and suggest some ways to overcome them.

This is not meant to be a textbook on Enrollment Management techniques. We are more concerned with advancing EM *theory* in this book than with filling in the details of EM *practice*. Reducing theory to practice is what we do every day in our work with clients. Our intent is to prime the pump of an ongoing conversation that we hope will continue online at our website and in other forums. From that conversation, we further hope that the ideas presented here will be refined, enriched and augmented with new conceptual insights and real-world examples.

A Note of Caution Before You Begin

We feel obliged to warn you that strewn across the pages that follow, like so many verbal supplements, are some pretty outrageous puns. Most, but not all, of them are – in the spirit of our EM=C² title – examples of a kind of quasi-scientific or just plain self-indulgent wordplay. Anticipating the chorus of groans building to a deafening crescendo as the book unfolds, we can only beg your indulgence. What do you expect from the teaming of a former theoretical physicist-mathematician and an unreconstructed Harvard *Lampoon* editor-cartoonist?

Jack Maguire and Larry Butler
Concord, Massachusetts
Fall 2008

Chapter 1

Original Synergies

The history of Enrollment Management dates back to 1973 BC (Boston College), where institutional crisis gave rise to some powerful insights about how synergies among previously isolated functions and activities might hold the key to institutional renewal.

In 1973, Boston College was in trouble, to put it mildly. A school with the rather modest status but lengthy history as a regional commuter college was running chronic deficits. Faculty salaries were frozen and the future looked bleak. A 25 percent national decline in high school graduates was being projected – 45 percent within the region of the country from which BC recruited most of its students. Low retention rates were a glaring issue and the financial impact of lost students reverberated throughout the institution in the form of greater freshman recruitment costs and a financial aid budget crunch. With a total endowment of only $5 million, the College was considered to have negative net assets. To say that BC faced an uphill battle towards solvency would be a serious understatement.

It was into the deep end of this turbulent fiscal pool that Frank Campanella, Executive Vice President and professor of finance at the

College, and Jack Maguire, Dean of Admissions and a mathematical physics professor, jumped (or more precisely, were pushed) when BC handed them the daunting mission of turning things around, if they could.

Synergy, data, and collaboration became the new watchwords. Despite limited available resources and looming financial threats, BC had many well-functioning units, including Admissions. But, they were isolated silos. At the time, the financial aid packages for incoming freshmen were awarded by Admissions and the packages for returning students were awarded separately by the Financial Aid Office. There was little interplay between the financial aid budgets for the incoming class and upperclassmen. In fact, the Admissions office was bringing in one third of the students and only receiving one quarter of the budget. The staffs of Admissions, Financial Aid, and the Registrar's Office had no history of coordinating their respective efforts. In order for operations to function more efficiently, all of this needed to change, and fast.[2]

To grapple with these vexing financial and organizational issues, Maguire and Campanella created a new research and marketing capability. Through the use of data, extensive research, and analysis, they began to bring the organization together by identifying critical trends, unflinchingly comparing Boston College's performance to that of its competitors, developing meaningful metrics and questionnaires, and putting into place a sophisticated admissions rating system that BC still uses today.

The new team had to get the financial aid budget under control, so they began examining the mathematical predictors of the tendencies of prospective students in different market segments to enroll at different net-pricing levels. This allowed the team to figure out how to make better admission decisions and use their modest recruiting and financial aid budgets more wisely. These early efforts became the underpinnings of the econometric modeling of enrollment outcomes frequently employed in enrollment management structures today.

Seemingly against all odds, with a newfound cohesion among admissions, financial aid, research, customer service, and marketing, the institution took off. Within a few short years, admissions applications rose dramatically, as did full-time undergraduate enrollment. BC achieved financial stability and developed a strong national reputation. As one inside observer commented: "It was incredible. Suddenly, Boston College was at the forefront."

EM Gets Its Name

The concept of Enrollment Management first appeared in print in the Fall 1976 issue of Boston College's *Bridge* Magazine. Jack Maguire's original article, "To the Organized Go the Students" (infelicitously titled by the magazine's editors and not the author) put forward the major premises and underlying ideas of Enrollment Management as they were being developed at BC.

As described in that article: "Enrollment Management is a process that brings together often disparate functions having to do with recruiting, funding, tracking, retaining, and replacing students as they move toward, within and away from the University."[3]

At the time, the notion of combining all of these functions was novel, to say the least. It had been developed under crisis conditions and used to address Boston College's many challenges in the early to mid-1970's. But the words describing BC's concerns would not look out of place in an article written by a typical Dean of Admissions or Enrollment today. The *Bridge* piece spoke of how BC officials – fearful of declining student demographics (a very ominous threat at the time as compared to a worrisome but less serious threat facing us today), low student retention rates, and a new wave of student transfers – were compelled to explore broader strategies to address the difficulties of succeeding in an increasingly competitive and complex higher education landscape.

The systemic hurdles described in 1976 are equally relatable to our present day experience. Skyrocketing operating costs and tuitions, distaste for the notion of "marketing" in educational circles, and the persistence of departmental silos struggling to coordinate their functions with one another have all been cited as major roadblocks. In the environment of the mid-1970s, the new framework opened up people's imaginations and a wealth of new opportunities. Enrollment Management offered both an innovative conceptual paradigm as well as a set of practical tools to address each of these issues.

EM Gains Adherents and New Thinkers

The Boston College success story certainly demonstrates the value of Enrollment Management philosophy and practice. Since then, EM concepts have spread across the nation. Many of today's experts in what is now a robust and dynamic profession were never connected directly with Boston College but encountered the paradigm years later, as it was being spread at early College Board conferences, in journal articles, and in practice at other institutions.

Numerous EM practitioners have developed their own notions of the profession, their own strategies, and their own ways of addressing the challenges common to today's colleges and universities. Many learned and eventually expanded on key concepts based on their own analyses and experiences.[4] Some details may differ, but the success of the original ideas lives on in the careers of numerous EM professionals who have achieved well-deserved acclaim.[5]

EM Evolves

It took more than two decades for Enrollment Management to permeate the slow-changing world of higher education and gain the traction that it has today. Though colleges and universities were frequently in need of new ideas, basic EM principles remained underutilized for quite a while. Some attribute EM's slow growth to structural impediments and its rapid expansion in recent years to the development of enterprise database systems like Banner and PeopleSoft. Whatever the contributing factors, during the 1990's and 2000's, Enrollment Management evolved into one of the most powerful and influential management paradigms in higher education.

Enrollment Management, in practice, has also adjusted to changing realities in the marketplace and within the institutions themselves. As competition between higher education institutions has intensified, EM has increasingly taken on the trappings of marketing, including the "sales funnel" metaphor and all of marketing's other, now-familiar tools and techniques: market research, modeling, positioning, branding, etc.

Has Marketing Become the "M" in EM?

41% of admissions/enrollment officers say they spend a "high" or "very high" amount of their time on developing marketing materials and another **35%** say they spend a "moderate" amount of time on this activity.

Findings from: Admissions/Enrollment Officers Survey 2008

The position of Enrollment Manager (most of them titled Vice President or Dean of Enrollment Management) has come to the fore in coordinating and overseeing these multifaceted marketing efforts.[6] As a result, Enrollment Management has become the lead administrative function shaping the public face, messaging, and student bodies at countless schools.

But with increasing institutional sophistication around matters of marketing has come a realization that not all aspects of a college or university's story are being captured through the EM lens. More and more, we are beginning to see a kind of functional re-siloing, as schools hire Marketing VPs (and increasingly Marketing-Communications VPs) with a full array of specialized skills who function as peers of the Enrollment Management VPs. This could be seen as a troubling development if adding a new position means that cross-functional collaboration is reduced. We are not advocating that the position of Enrollment Management VP necessarily be the senior *position* to which all others report, but rather that the *discipline* of Enrollment Management be reflected in Marketing and Communications and throughout the enterprise.

There is, of course, a natural partnership between Enrollment Management and Marketing – one that Maguire Associates has long encouraged. So long as marketing is not simplistically defined and practiced as merely institutional promotion but includes the ongoing analysis and substantive improvement of the institutional "product" to fulfill the value propositions and promises made to prospective students, the partnership between Marketing and EM can be one of those great synergies that serve the institution extremely well.

Unfortunately, in far too many institutions, Enrollment Management has become more about competing with other schools over increasing applications and boosting yield; and less about finding the best fit between college and student to the lasting benefit of both. EM, in other words, has for some schools become a tool for short-term gain and tactical advantage at the expense of long-term strategic distinctiveness. As a consequence, we've witnessed a backlash in recent years against EM, which many view as a commercial wolf in non-profit sheep's clothing that deploys an array of slick public relations tactics to promote the commoditization of higher education.

We take strong issue with this characterization but believe that it will persist so long as Enrollment Management is allowed to become synonymous with Marketing. EM, if we can recapture its "original synergies" and then re-imagine it as an institution-wide discipline, has the potential to go far beyond being one component of a marketing/communications strategy.

Whither EM's Original Synergies?
Some synergies that were terribly important to those of us who toiled early on in the vineyards of Enrollment Management seem somehow to defy full integration into the EM paradigm.

- **Retention is still orphaned.** At Boston College, student retention was an integral part of the enrollment management system from the beginning. Today, most schools are acutely aware of the importance of retention. In fact, some are beginning to assign responsibility for retention, typically in terms of student "engagement" and student "affairs," to the chief enrollment officer. Examples of this include Northeastern University's recent appointment of a Vice President of Enrollment and Student Affairs, and New England College's hiring a Vice President for Enrollment and Student Engagement. By its nature, retention is a desirable outcome, not a discrete activity or administrative function. Indeed, a big part of the student experience (including whether or not the student persists) is shaped by faculty advisors, academic counselors, athletic coaches, extracurricular mentors, and fellow students. With responsibility for student retention so broadly distributed, it's not difficult to understand why it has so long been an orphaned component of EM.

Concerned About Retention

As a group, presidents rated Student Retention as their second-highest concern among 29 issues facing academic institutions - issues involving faculty, students, and finances as well as enrollment and other topics. (Highest was Rising Health Care Costs.)

74% of presidents rated Student Retention as a "significant concern" at their institutions.*

* "Significant Concern" are ratings of 4 and 5 in a scale where 1 = Not a Concern to 5 = Very Great Concern).

Findings from: Presidents Survey 2005

- **Faculty and alumni are out of the loop.** Less easy to fathom is why faculty and alumni so often remain out of the loop when it comes to the practice of Enrollment Management. Both groups were very much in the loop "back in the day." In fact, one of the most successful initiatives at BC was the deployment of the FAST – Faculty Alumni Student Team – to augment the College's recruitment efforts. By expanding the school's recruiting staff ten-fold at no cost to the institution, the FAST was instrumental in increasing applications by 200 percent and enrollments by 20 percent by the early 1980s. Notwithstanding the resistance of faculty groups to the expansion of non-teaching duties, especially if uncompensated, there are still opportunities to more creatively involve faculty in EM's broader mission, not only with respect to student recruitment but also with alumni fundraising (more on this in Chapter 9.) Colleges and universities that don't see that potential are in danger of losing their faculties in more ways than one.

Why is there so little collaboration across the graduation boundary? One of the most surprising findings of our recent survey of senior Admissions and Enrollment Officers (in partnership with the *Chronicle of Higher Education*) is the apparent decline in the use of alumni volunteers over the last 10 to 20 years. Senior Admissions and Enrollment Officers with more than 20 years of experience have made much more frequent use of alumni in the recruitment and yield-enhancement functions than those with fewer than five years of experience. Officers who are younger and newer to the field have relied more on technology, with extraordinary advances in use of the Web, while their senior counterparts have had less opportunity (and possibly less inclination) to use the newest electronic technology.

Alumni Involvement in Recruiting

Only 15% of admissions/enrollment officers say their offices engage alumni "quite a lot" or "very much" in recruiting undergraduates.

Findings from: Admissions/Enrollment Officers Survey 2008

The Biggest Synergy of All

This last point brings us to our overall assessment of the recent evolution of Enrollment Management as one which often appears to be moving away from, rather than closer to, the original synergies that lay at the heart of the concept when it was first formulated over 30 years ago at Boston College.

Those synergies were found most obviously in the integration and coordination of the work of enrollment-related functions that previously were pursued independently. Viewed more closely, however, one could see other synergies at play in the crafting of coherent institutional messaging and, most importantly, the creation of strategic alignment at all levels throughout the institution. All of this rested upon a strong leadership commitment to building interpersonal and cross-functional collaboration.

If there is one dimension of synergy that concerns us today, it is the stubborn persistence of the silo culture. This has not been so much a case of institutions defaulting back to silos as much as their never having transcended that operating style in the first place. Perhaps it takes an existential crisis of the scale Boston College faced in the 1970s to overcome the tendency toward a rigid, departmental mindset. We have seen enough cases of talented leaders who have effected such a cultural transformation in the absence of a major crisis to know that it is possible. We also know that cultural change is a necessary precondition to everything else that Enrollment Management at its best can achieve. Certainly, it is essential to the reformulation of EM we propose in this book.

If Enrollment Management's full potential has yet to be realized or if some of EM's "original synergies" are difficult to discern in contemporary practice, the problem is not so much with Enrollment Management *per se*, but with the fact that as a professional discipline it has not adapted to dramatic changes in the higher education marketplace. In the next chapter we will address one of those dramatic changes: the emergence of powerful third party influencers like *US News* and their college rankings which have established a false but dominating context in which institutional leaders often find themselves acting against their own – and their students' – best interests. Breaking out of the debilitating rankings mindset is essential if Enrollment Management is to recapture the promise of its original synergies and move to the next level of effectiveness.

Chapter 2

Rankingdom Rules

Where once institutions were independent fiefdoms free to set their own rules, they now find themselves struggling to compete for students and funds in a realm where US News and other third parties rank them into making self-defeating decisions.

Welcome to Rankingdom! Yes, we all live there now – in a realm where the rankers make the rules. The all-powerful ran-king, of course, is *US News and World Report*. A few other guidebook publications[7] that compile annual rankings of colleges and universities and the various survey and testing services[8] that generate comparative institutional data comprise the nobility. Taken together, this royal family has become the dominant source of third-party influence on the college choices of prospective students and their families.

We want to be clear about this: As a tool for encouraging colleges to improve academic quality and enhance the substantive value of their very expensive product, comparative data can serve a legitimate and beneficial purpose – benchmarking against other schools, identifying best practices, and so on. We advise our clients to do this all the time.

However, the problem with rankings is that they fuel a preoccupation with school status in the competitive battle for students. As a consequence, institutional leaders feel they have little choice but to play the rankings game or risk losing this all-important annual battle. Toward that end, they invest their energies and scarce resources in short-term, tactical efforts to improve their ranking scores. What they should be doing – and what we believe Enrollment Management should be all about – is focusing on sharpening their school's distinctive mission and seeking to build lifelong relationships with students and alumni to whom that mission best appeals and serves. In Rankingdom, there is precious little incentive to adopt such a mission-sensitive, long-term strategic course and plenty of pressure to accede to the power of the Royal Rankers.

Abdicating the Metrics Throne

Before we get too upset about this sorry state of affairs, though, we must acknowledge the harsh truth: colleges and universities, to a considerable extent, have brought this upon themselves[9]. They missed their opportunity some 20 years ago to frame the discussion about the metrics of higher education. Had the institutions seized that opportunity at the moment when *US News & World Report's Rating the Colleges* (1984) or *The Best Colleges in America* (1985) introduced the rankings with a sputtering start, using only reputational measures to rank institutions, and not abdicated their natural claim to the metrics throne, *they* would have been the ones to determine what to measure, how to define quality, and what to consider optimal outcomes.

For example, had they early on empowered an independent professional organization to provide these data in an objective but educationally relevant format, a different scenario might well have transpired – one that left no vacuum into which *US News* could maneuver. Envision a scenario in which *US News* and other publishing companies never perceived the ranking of colleges to be a viable business or never saw their rankings catch on because something like a "National Association of Colleges and Universities Research Center" was already out front providing the public with concrete institutional assessment data to complement the qualitative and promotional information provided by the institutions themselves.[9] Once it became clear that the public was clamoring for the information, higher education could have discouraged *US News'* annual entry or at the very least, rendered it less visible, less unique, and less profitable.

As it stands, *US News* has established the *de facto* metrics for the national dialog, and to the extent that institutions cannot separate their own priorities from those established by this third party, they play out a very rational, yet troubling, response: They set institutional priorities based on what is being measured.

Instead of a school determining what it cares most about, what is central to its mission, and measuring *those* things carefully and publicly, it measures and invests in what *US News* has determined to be the universal values to which all schools should subscribe. By measuring the same elements for all institutions, the implication, deliberate or not, is that they all should be doing the same things, regardless of their differing missions and values, and regardless of the particular interests and needs of their respective constituencies.

It's pretty clear that in Rankingdom the metrics tail is too often wagging the institutional dog. What is not clear is whether the old dog can learn some new metrics.

Unprincipled Certainty

Reducing the practice of Enrollment Management to a preoccupation with winning competitive advantage is perhaps the most depressing but not the only consequence of the rankings mindset. Like Heisenberg's "uncertainty principle," the rankings end up distorting the very nature of the reality under observation – as those being observed attempt to game the system to their advantage and, in so doing, shift their institutional priorities in ways they otherwise would not.

A more accurate term might be "unprincipled certainty," because even as *US News* defends the statistical validity of their numbers, they acknowledge that their metrics cannot fully measure subtle institutional differences nor, for that matter, the true relative quality of often vastly different academic experiences. Their rankings represent exactly what *US News* says they represent: They measure only what they measure.[10] A true statement, as far as it goes, but somewhat disingenuous.

What *US News* measures it also affects. Intentionally or not, legitimate tools of statistical analysis have become intimidating bludgeons of perceived authority. The rankings have gone from being comparative measurements of a few selected features of a college to being a "scientific" formula that somehow separates the mediocre from the good, the good from the better, and the better from the best.

Called "specious formulas and spurious precision" by at least one well-respected educator[11], the *US News* rankings are problematic in several ways. They accentuate relatively small differences between institutions, yet they create what appears to be a tangible rationale for defining institutional success and failure – notwithstanding the fact that the publishers themselves discourage such use by institutions as well as by students and their families. State legislators and commissions of higher education also take these "quality" rankings seriously and use them to make judgments about the return on their investments of state funds in support of public higher education.

Admissions Officers Generally Hold a Negative View of the Rankings

When asked how they would rate the impact of College Rankings on "the admissions practices" of their institutions, over four times more admissions/enrollment officers gave a negative than a positive rating.

48% cited a "somewhat negative" or "very negative" impact, while 10% cited a "somewhat positive" or "very positive" impact.

Findings from: Admissions/Enrollment Officers Survey 2008

Double Bind Studies

In Rankingdom, college presidents find themselves in a classic double bind. Either they pledge their fealty to the rankings or risk the erosion of institutional reputation and loss of competitive standing. In a kind of race to the bottom, many college presidents and boards believe they are obliged to play the rankings game and, in some cases, bend the system just to stay competitive.

Manipulation of SAT (or ACT) scores is a case in point that illustrates an embedded double bind lurking within the larger context of the rankings. Because it is one of the *US News* variables, the average SAT score of enrolled students has taken on unprecedented importance. While simply changing a school's SAT average might not in itself change its ranking, the statistical relationship between SAT scores and college rank is compelling.[12]

Do SAT Scores Gauge Preparedness?

Despite their importance in the college rankings, SAT/ACT scores are not viewed by college faculty as strongly indicative of college preparation. 57% of college faculty "agree" and only 9% "strongly agree" with the notion that SAT or ACT scores are good indicators of the preparedness of students for the academic demands of their institutions.

Findings from: Teachers and Faculty Survey 2006

Not surprisingly, some institutions have developed strategies to admit and enroll students with ever-higher scores. Some try to improve their SAT average through the selective use of so-called "merit aid." But using merit aid merely to make SAT numbers look good can actually be self-defeating. While such non-need-based aid, thoughtfully and strategically deployed, is a valuable tool for institutions that lack billions in endowment funds to compete with their better-heeled counterparts, it can have unintended consequences if used as a short-term fix. In at least one instance, a college had been "chasing prestige" by discounting its tuition heavily through the use of merit aid only to find that the resulting erosion in net tuition revenues so constrained operating budgets that it undercut the college's ability to fulfill its promise to the very students attracted by the merit aid.[13]

Even a school that doesn't use merit aid as part of its recruitment strategy is likely to make glowing promises about academic and campus life in order to lure high-achieving students away from more selective competitors. Living up to those promises, however, may require major resource infusions to upgrade academic quality and campus infrastructure. Failure to make those investments can lead rather quickly to lower retention and lower student and alumni satisfaction – more problems than the school probably faced before ramping up student "quality." Worse still, entering students whose expectations have been raised only to feel misled are more likely to transfer out (or persist in an increasingly dissatisfied state) and end up poisoning the recruitment pool long into the future, as they share their negative opinions with siblings, friends, and untold numbers of visitors to MySpace, College Confidential, and the larger blogosphere.

Thus, we have an SAT double bind within the rankings double bind. Institutions can either pursue high SAT scores to improve their ranking and, if they fail to fulfill their promises, risk alienating influential students and their families over the long term; or institutions don't pursue high SAT scores and risk a loss of reputational status and a decline in applications, enrollments and tuition revenue over the short term.[14]

For most schools with high levels of tuition dependency, a highly competitive marketplace would seem to necessitate the enrollment of paying students, not just those receiving large institutional grant awards. So the vicious cycle continues, making it even more difficult to unilaterally disarm. Spurred on by media reports and internal pressures from trustees, alumni and faculty infatuated with prestige or legitimately concerned with financial solvency, institutions find it that much riskier to get off the rankings treadmill than to stay on it. And it gets worse. With each new round of rankings, as schools seek to gain and maintain a competitive edge, the rankings themselves are validated yet again. As the perceived significance of the rankings grows[15], those participating institutions that improve their positions become complicit in promoting the prevailing view by proudly displaying their ranking kudos in promotional materials.[16].

Students and their families also fuel the process by literally buying into the false value-for-money tradeoff. "If we're going to spend that much money for a college education, it better buy us prestige." Thus do applicant and school, each drinking from the same cup of rankings Kool-Aid, end up making irrevocable decisions that may actually undermine their respective best interests.

The Way Out? Go Inside!

Fortunately, there *is* a way out of Rankingdom. But for many it will seem counterintuitive in the extreme. The way to get out is to go in! Here are the three keys to get *out* of the kingdom.

- **Go inside the rankings and take what you need.** The rankings aren't going away. So adopt them for your institution's own purposes. Deconstruct the factors in the ranking formula and devise ways of maximizing performance on those that have the greatest bearing on your academic product and your students' experience. Use these selected factors to assess your institution's performance against internally derived benchmarks or against the peer or aspirant institutions of your own choice. The resulting comparative analyses can motivate positive institutional changes. For example, student retention and graduation rates play a significant role in the ranking formula, but they are also metrics of major interest to institutional leaders, whether or not third-party rankings ever existed. Think of it as using *their* ranking system to create your own – one in which your institution is constantly improving, the better to thrive within its own niche.

- **Go inside your institutional identity and embrace it.** After all, the evolution of species is not about the survival of the biggest or survival of the best but of the fittest – the fittest within a particular environmental niche or ecosystem.

  In order to flourish within its niche, a college needs to understand clearly: a) how the relevant ecosystem operates, b) what other "species" share that ecosystem and compete (and/or co-operate) within it, and most importantly, c) the college's own distinctive characteristics and advantageous adaptations.

  Every institution has the power to define specifically what distinguishes it from other institutions – what values it holds most dear, how it goes about teaching, what it seeks to achieve on behalf of its students, and what kinds of students it hopes to serve – in short, its institutional DNA. Armed with this self-knowledge and with the aid of sophisticated market research and analytical tools, schools can now identify with much greater precision the prospective students most likely to share these same values and interests, and thus most likely to apply and enroll. As a result, colleges don't have to game the system and compromise their principles to attract an entering class. Third-party rankings become less relevant when it becomes possible for the first and second parties (the school and the student) to co-create a ranking system of their own – defined by the institution's unique DNA of mission and values.

- **Go inside the rankings castle and peek behind the curtain of power.** One variable that US News fails to include in its ranking formula may actually be an even better predictor of institutional rank than many which they do include: endowment value per student. Just try this instructive little experiment. Compile a list of the 20 private colleges and universities with the largest endowments. Then take a look at the US News ranking of the 20 Top National Universities. You guessed it – the same schools appear on both lists[17]. The recent outcry in newspaper op-ed pages, professional journals, the blogosphere and government hearing rooms has brought long overdue public attention to the wealth that has accumulated in the endowments of a handful of the nation's most selective institutions, even as the price of tuition has spiraled out of reach of the average family.[18]

A Trustee's Concern About the Tuition Gap

"Rapidly rising tuitions are helping to widen the social divide, leaving so many folks behind, the nation is becoming weaker. We need to solve this problem, and make college affordable to all – perhaps more public funds."

Comments from: College Governing Board Members Survey 2007

But the clamor for these institutions to use more of their wealth to moderate the cost of education for financially strapped families has really only revealed a part of the story. What is not being addressed is the fact that elite institutions with huge endowments are already heavily discounting their tuitions by infusing their operating budgets with hundreds of millions of endowment dollars. Doing so allows them not only to offer far richer financial-aid packages[19] but also to set their sticker prices well below the true cost of the education they provide their students. The students at elite colleges have access to more accomplished professors (attracted by higher salaries), a wider array of courses, smaller class sizes, larger and more comprehensive library systems, and other amenities than the less well-to-do colleges with similar tuition sticker prices can offer. Thus, those wealthier institutions attract a disproportionate share of smart, wealthy students – who later, as powerful and wealthy alumni, further feed those already bloated endowments by "bringing more sand to the beach." In short, the massive endowments of elite universities confer on them an unassailable competitive advantage in the form of a hidden discount that forces the less-well-endowed institutions to try to manipulate the rankings and compromise their principles in a scramble for a limited pool of the most talented and most diverse students.

The Overburdened Underendowed

Less well-endowed institutions struggle with burdens that the elite schools do not, as noted by the president of a 4-year college in 2005:

"Morally, higher education is in a bad place .... less than 15% of ... students [in schools with the largest endowments] are Pell-eligible.[20] So for a president like me trying to raise funds for an HBCU* where over 80% of the students are Pell eligible, it is tough. Philanthropists are helping the rich get richer, which means we'll have more Americans who won't be able to attend college, [as] schools like mine raise tuition to try to offer a reasonable living wage for faculty and staff. The richest schools get the best faculty as well, while the students with the most need get the leftovers."

* Historically Black Colleges and Universities

Comments from: College Presidents Survey 2005

Knowledge is power. Once they become aware of the futility of trying to offer a richer product at a comparable net price than those deep-pocketed elite institutions with huge endowments, the leaders of most other colleges and universities will have the power to withstand the intense pressure to play the rankings game. They will know that the system operates like a casino where the house of the heavily endowed always wins. Only those in the top tier of selective schools with discretionary endowment funds can really afford to gamble on, or for that matter, have much of a stake in, the year-to-year ranking shifts. All the other players would do well to simply cash in their chips and leave the casino.

It's Hard to Compete with the Perceived Need to Compete with the Highly Endowed Schools

One enrollment officer expressed frustration with the prevailing competitive "frenzy":

"It is most frustrating that all assumptions about the process that the press/media ... reports as being the state of the industry today are applicable only to fewer than 30 institutions in the country compared to the reality of the other 3,600 institutions. They have created a totally false state of frenzy and panic among students and parents in a world in which there are so many outstanding colleges and universities from which to choose – most better than the namebrands for most undergraduates."

Comments from: Admissions/Enrollment Officers Survey 2008

As an institutional leader, you already possess the three keys to breaking out of the rankings-fueled vicious cycle.

- **The Self-Measurement Key** that allows you to go inside the rankings and take from them only that which will make your institution stronger.

- **The Self-Knowledge Key** that allows you to embrace your distinctive identity and unleash its power to inspire and build loyal student and alumni communities for the long term.

- **The System Understanding Key** that allows you to see clearly who controls the levers of power in Rankingdom and thereby free yourself of false illusions that limit your options.

You now hold the keys to Rankingdom. Take them, unlock the gates, and flee!

Chapter 3

Is That Your Funnel Answer?

Turns out, that good old, reliable metaphor – the enrollment funnel – is leaking like a sieve. And if not to hold conceptual water, what's a metaphor?

Many institutional leaders, confounded by the painful double binds of Rankingdom described in the previous chapter, are grasping for insights, methods and tools that will restore some measure of control over a process that is becoming more complex and – too often – chaotic with each passing enrollment cycle. But the tools within closest reach are no longer right for the task. In this chapter we discuss perhaps the single most familiar organizing principle in the EM toolbox – the Enrollment Funnel – and ask whether there may be something beyond this metaphor that can better serve our institutional needs.

The Funnel's Business Origins
Like many concepts used in the nonprofit sector, the Enrollment Funnel (Figure 3-1) so familiar to folks in the college enrollment field was borrowed from the world of business, where it is still referred to

as the Marketing (or Sales) Funnel. In that conceptualization, Prospects enter the wide end; some of them are transformed into Leads; and some of these are carefully nurtured into Qualified Leads who display a greater likelihood of being converted into Customers.

With its connotation of a narrowing flow of individuals who are increasingly disposed to make a positive purchase decision, the funnel image resonates with the actual experience of drawing a stream of paying customers to the vendor's enterprise. It also demarcates phases along the way, as the truly "qualified" prospect or lead is accorded more focused marketing attention in an effort to convert the qualified into the committed.

Figure 3-1
The Traditional Enrollment Funnel

In the same way, higher education's version of the marketing funnel conveys the notion of a directed and increasingly targeted flow of prospective students into the institutional embrace of a particular college or university. The Enrollment Funnel employs a different set of terms but shares the same principle. For "lead," substitute "inquirer." For "qualified lead," substitute "applicant." Things get a bit more complicated at the final "customer" conversion stage, though, where in the college version the sale is not actually consummated when the applicant is "admitted," but rather when the admitted student accepts admission and confirms that acceptance with a deposit. Even then, the sale is not fully booked until the individual enrolls and matriculates. And that's just enrollment for the first year or semester. Continuation (or persistence) through multiple semesters and years all the way through completion of a degree is now considered the true outlet point from the enrollment funnel.

Back in the days before the emergence of Enrollment Management, when the admissions office worked in relative isolation from the financial aid and registrar's offices, the very concept of a single enrollment funnel – with its implicit recognition of a phased flow of students – would have been seen as an alien notion, something artificially transplanted from the world of commerce and grafted onto a very different kind of organism. Private higher education back then was an exclusive enclave with gatekeepers guarding the entrance – certainly not marketers seeking out and encouraging prospective students to apply.

A Trustee's Take on Business Models

"Institutions of higher education have uncritically adopted market and business based models of decision-making that have tended to erode the distinctive intellectual function of higher education. Attention needs to be given to the development of different decision models that will better embody and respect the distinctive role of universities in society."

Comments from: College Governing Board Members Survey 2007

The Multiple Funnel Model - A Welcome Advance

For some time now, we have recognized certain inadequacies in the Single Funnel Model. For one thing, it suggests a passive flow (subject only to "gravitational" forces) that visually leaves no space for institutional agency in encouraging the movement of individuals from one stage to the next. It describes a closed system with no entry points for flows that bypass earlier phases. And the funnel outlet is typically at the confirmed enrollment stage. We all know that student retention is critical, but the single funnel doesn't really reflect this. Nor does it allow for post-graduation stages in the relationship of an alumnus with the school.

By contrast, a Multiple Funnels Model (Figure 3-2) depicts a series of funnels that encompasses a student's entire lifespan in relation to the institution. This lifespan continues beyond graduation into what might called a Stewardship phase when, as an alumnus, the former student becomes a source of ongoing institutional support.

Most students will start as prospects. Some prospects will then choose to become inquirers. Some inquirers will choose to become applicants. A vast majority will choose not to pass through the very first funnel. Others will introduce themselves into the system without being part of a preceding funnel, such as a student who applies for admission without any previous contact (the so-called "stealth applicant") or, far less frequently, a generous donor who was never before associated with the institution.

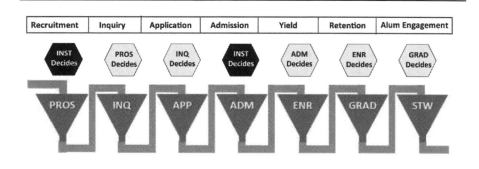

Figure 3-2
The Multiple Funnel Model

At other points in the cycle, it is impossible for an individual to appear without having been present in a previous funnel. For instance, students cannot be admitted to the institution without having first applied and cannot enroll without having been admitted.

As shown in Figure 3-2, this series of funnels tracks well with the multiple EM phases. The recruitment phase begins when an institution acquires prospective student names and contacts them through a search campaign or when prospective students express interest in the institution as inquirers. The recruitment phase ends after students apply to the institution, then the admission phase commences, followed by the yield, retention, and alumni engagement phases.

Throughout the course of the relationship, the student/alumnus controls nearly all stages of the process. Of the seven major decision points, the institution controls only two (the choice of whom to consider a prospect and whom to admit).[21] In fact, any student who chooses to do so can circumvent the first or second funnel, initiate the relationship as an inquirer or applicant, and eliminate the first institutionally-controlled decision.

The Multiple Funnel Model has a number of advantages over the traditional Single Funnel:

- By allowing for the depiction of conversion points between successive funnels, it highlights the school's role in influencing those conversion decisions in ways that meet institutional needs.

- It opens up the system to allow for the introduction of new entrants (stealth applicants, transfers.)

- It extends Enrollment Management to include post-graduation stages and lifelong relationships with the school.

- Adopting a view of "enrollment" as entering into lifelong relationships with the school thus frees us to consider time periods longer than the coming year's class and populations other than those matriculating in that class.

- This total lifespan model expands market opportunities for the institution while at the same time extending life enrichment opportunities for the individual.

- Cultivating these relationships implies a goal of maximizing total net lifetime support of the institution and not simply net tuition revenue at the point of enrollment.

Finally, a series of funnels imputes a degree of proactivity, agency, and momentum to the student/alum that the traditional funnel does not. The conventional image suggests that if you push enough numbers into the top, you'll get the results you want out the bottom. The multiple funnels model better lends itself to the far more realistic idea that, unless you provide enough reason for a student to traverse the distance from the previous funnel to the next, you can fill the funnel with as many prospects as you want, and you might still end up with very little exiting the other end.

A Metaphorical Defect

Even this multiple funnel concept, for all of its improvements on the single funnel model, does not fully depict what is actually happening in the marketplace.

Think about it. In a real funnel, all of the material entering the broad opening at the top eventually flows out the narrow outlet at the bottom. As a metaphor for a winnowing process, the funnel is inherently defective because it makes no provision for the outflows of those who do not proceed through subsequent phases. The focus continues to be on those who choose (or are selected) to move through successive phases; not on those who never enter or who flow out of the system.

If this were simply a matter of symbolic nitpicking, we would not be pushing the point; after all, everybody basically gets what the funnel image means. But more is at stake than symbolism. *The funnel metaphor actually perpetuates a crucial blind spot in the way enrollment managers and other institutional leaders view the world.* It is a view that, like the funnel image itself, narrows down to a preoccupation with enrolling a class, often at the expense of assuring the optimal match of students and school, never mind building lifelong relationships.

Demise of the Recruitment Funnel

"I would say the most significant challenge facing admissions is the changing nature of our admissions procedures. The recruitment funnel no longer exists and students approach institutions of higher education when they are ready (often using the application as the first point of inquiry)."

Comments from: Admissions/Enrollment Officers Survey 2008

The Dark Matters

The vast bulk of the enrollment universe is hidden from view, but that's where the real opportunities are. Think of all the populations who flow out of (or never enter) the enrollment funnel(s):

- High school students who never become prospects
- Prospects who never inquire
- Inquirers who do not apply
- Applicants who never inquired ("stealth applicants")
- Applicants who are not admitted
- Admits who do not enroll
- Enrollees who do not persist or graduate
- Graduates who do not become engaged alumni

These "opt-out" (or "never-opted-in") populations vastly outnumber those who by choice or selection *do* flow through each of the conversion points. These populations are like the so-called "dark matter" that cosmologists say represents the great bulk of the mass in the universe. And like the dark matter, these populations are largely invisible, even though they are right in front of us all the time. In some cases, institutions choose not to see them. For example, take those never targeted as prospects in the first place. Most of the other prospects *were* identified, but because they did not convert to the next phase, they are neither tracked nor followed up. They are off the radar screens because they do not seem to have any practical value or relevance to the outcome that is so ardently sought – namely, enrolling students in this coming year's class. Maintaining focus on those who do pass through each of the funnels on the way to and through matriculation would seem to be more than enough of a burden to overworked enrollment staff.

Growth in Stealth Applicants

77% of admissions/enrollment officers say that the number of stealth applicants at their institutions has grown "somewhat" or "greatly" during the past decade.

Findings from: Admissions/Enrollment Officers Survey 2008

To be sure, the choice to neglect a particular population is not always a conscious one. There is a real component of developmental awareness involved here. Think of Jim Carrey's character in the film *The Truman Show*, a man so embedded in an artificially constructed world that it takes a cataclysmic event from the outside to alert him to the truth that he is actually living in a world within a larger world. Disengaging from a framework so mentally ingrained is not as simple as being informed of a larger world out there. It may require reframing one's entire conception of what it means to do Enrollment Management. There is likely to be some energetic pushback against so drastic a notion.

Does the dark matter? Do these invisible populations really justify the expenditure of already scarce resources on monitoring and reaching out to them? We believe these "dark" populations really do matter for two very compelling reasons.

- **They can teach us.** There is much to be learned from those who choose not to respond positively to the institution's value propositions and messaging, or to its offers of admission and financial support, or, for that matter, to the actual academic and other experiences it provides. All of these opt-out populations at every stage represent a vast repository of geo-demographics, opinions, preferences, and attitudes which, if tapped, could help to shape and refine the institution's propositions, messages, offerings, and substantive reality. Even if only to confirm that those opting out are not those whom we would have wanted to decide in our favor, or to confirm the efficacy of our recruitment and enrollment efforts, shining the light of analysis on these dark matter populations would yield many valuable insights – both tactical and strategic.

- **They are markets.** These populations continue to be audiences and potential markets for the school's programs and services. Applicants who aren't admitted may one day become adult learners. Accepts who don't enroll may one day become satisfied transfer students. Matriculants who don't persist may yet return to complete their studies or still become donors. There are any number of ways that inquirers (who by definition expressed some interest in the school at one time) may yet become supporters, referral sources, and influencers on behalf of the school, regardless of whether they themselves ever took subsequent steps beyond their initial inquiry. They may also have siblings and friends who are potential prospects.

The rest of this book is devoted to developing an alternative decision-making framework that moves beyond the funnel metaphor. We recognize, however, that the multiple funnel model is itself a substantial leap forward in conceptualizing an EM process – especially one with a lifespan dimension. We would not advise abandonment of such a robust and useful framework in favor of, figuratively, taking a shot in the dark. On the way to the new paradigm we have in mind, however, it just may be that moving from a single funnel to a multiple funnel worldview is a necessary step – a kind of conceptual stopover en route to an even broader paradigm. If you are still living in a single-funnel world, by all means adopt the multiple funnel conception, but don't get stuck there. A whole cosmos of communities awaits.

Chapter 4

EM=C²

It's time for a reformulation of Enrollment Management that embraces the new cosmology of multiple communities, virtual as well as physical.

In the previous chapter, we pointed out how the "funnel" metaphor that has served for so long to structure the thinking of EM practitioners is insufficient to address the needs of institutions trying to cope with the realities of today's world. This is a world in which virtual communities proliferate in cyberspace, global boundaries are erased, stealth applicants and other "dark matter" populations abound, and *US News*, MySpace, Facebook, and the blogosphere shape the expectations and opinions of those making college choices. But if it's not our "funnel" answer, what *is* our answer to how Enrollment Management can better function in this new world?

We propose a new way of thinking about EM. Instead of the traditional model of students flowing through sequential funnel stages leading to their enrollment and retention, we recommend a new model for building and leveraging a *community of communities* (including student communities) simultaneously and over an extended period of time.

Our Revised Formula: EM=C²

In a shameless reworking of Einstein's elegant formula, we have adopted EM=C² as our name for a new EM with Community at its core. EM=C² is about cultivating, nurturing, maintaining and leveraging communities, including communities of influence, as well as communities of students, advocates, donors, stewards, etc. Funnels are too Newtonian to describe this new world of multiple, on-line and on-ground communities. Instead, we need to think of EM in terms of modern physics with all of its uncertainty, simultaneity, and order within chaos – a complex, adaptive system that is dynamic, nonlinear, emergent and multidimensional.

In our new EM=C² formula:

- **E = Enrollment** redefined and broadened to describe, from the community member's perspective, a process of joining, experiencing, contributing to and transitioning from all kinds of virtual and physical communities.

- **M = Management** redefined and broadened to describe, from the institution's perspective, a process of understanding, inspiring, engaging and leveraging all kinds of virtual and physical communities.

- **C² = Community of Communities** where the institutional community is redefined as the current expression of the DNA of mission and values that inspire and hold together its affiliated communities over time.

When we speak of "enrollment" in this new model, we refer not merely to the process leading to admission, matriculation and graduation of a cohort of students, but rather to enrollment into a burgeoning array of communities beginning well before admission and extending long after graduation. And when we speak of "management," we refer not merely to a process of orchestrating the flows of students and others into their respective communities, but to a more nuanced, responsive, data-driven process of cultivating and shaping communities and their inter-relationships over time.

Returning to "C" Square One

With this new formulation of Enrollment Management, we are actually proposing a return to "square one." The noble enterprise we call higher education began, after all, as a coming together of two communities. A community of scholars "enrolled" a community of students and together they formed a community of communities – a learning community – where each learned from the other.

With each new enrolled student community and each new cadre of faculty and staff, donors, parents, trustees, and boosters – all comprising additional support communities – institutions of higher education grow and evolve over time, not only in size and scope but also in the historical depth of their reputations, achievements and legacies. Today's college or university is the sum total of all the affiliated communities that currently exist and all that came before.

$EM=C^2$ is not a novel construct derived from present-day realities imposed on the traditional model. Rather, we believe that coping with these new realities requires reaching back to recapture a far more durable truth. Education has always been about communities, the needs of their members, and their relationships with one another. The essence of C^2, then, is the synergistic power of communities to enhance one another and the institution with which they are all affiliated.

Communities Are Where You Find EM

Clay Shirkey, in his book *Here Comes Everybody*, provides a wealth of examples of distributed, self-empowered communities that form in cyberspace in ever-increasing numbers. Many of them mobilize on behalf of causes, circulate petitions, raise money, organize on-the-ground demonstrations, and exert intense pressure on institutional bureaucracies with remarkable effect and in amazingly rapid fashion. He calls this phenomenon "organizing without an organization."[22] Institutional leaders who don't recognize this phenomenon and build it into how they view and practice Enrollment Management are, to mix a metaphor, burying their heads in the sands of time.

In an Internet-worked world where virtual communities proliferate at an astonishing pace and third-party influence is pervasive, understanding and engaging communities of all kinds – not just the enrolled student community – is essential. The EM=C² model goes beyond the traditional notion of enrollment into student communities to include enrollment into communities that provide other critical benefits to the institution.

- ## Student/Client Communities

   Clearly, enrollment into student communities continues to be the centerpiece. All institutions, especially those that are highly dependent on tuition revenue, must of necessity have a continuing flow of students. Students are, after all, the lifeblood of the educational enterprise. But there are other client communities whose "enrollment" must be encouraged and sustained as well. These would include one-off purchasers and ongoing subscribers to the institution's educational and other products, whether they be publications, travel programs, athletic events, or other ancillary enterprises.

- ## Support Communities

   Colleges and universities require support of many kinds. Financial support beyond what is available through tuition and fees is the most obvious; this is typically the focus of the development or advancement office. The communities most frequently targeted are alumni donors, parents, corporations, foundations and the like. There are other forms of support, including: volunteers who assist in student recruitment or fundraising, people who serve on governing and advisory boards to lend their wisdom and expertise on subjects ranging from financial to academic; and fans and boosters of athletic programs who purchase tickets and t-shirts and support the institutional brand through their advocacy for the school and its teams. And then there are some communities, like the faculty and administrative staff, who also require recruitment and engagement in ways that will encourage their best efforts and deepen their commitment to the school over time.

• Reputational Communities

An institution's reputation is the sum total of a myriad of factors ranging from objectively measured assessments of the school's academic quality, to its historical legacy, to the most recent news items affecting public opinion. The management of reputation is a very real responsibility of institutional leaders, but it takes more than simply monitoring negative press and planting more positive stories. Leaders must also monitor the institution's "product" in all of its aspects and take all necessary steps to maintain and upgrade the quality of that product. (Of course, publicizing such substantive improvements has an honorable history in building a school's reputation.) But just as important are the steps institutions can take to build and maintain "enrollment" into communities that hold disproportionate sway over institutional reputation, including major employers of graduates, accrediting agencies, and professional associations. The leaders of peer institutions represent yet another community with considerable reputational influence.

• Goodwill Communities

A benefit even more intangible, perhaps, than reputation, is goodwill. Webster defines goodwill as "a kindly feeling of approval and support; benevolent interest or concern" and "the favor or advantage that [an enterprise] has acquired especially through its brands and its good reputation." There can be little doubt that in an age when there are so many forces at play in the marketplace and so many sources of influence affecting college choice, it is only good policy for a school to maximize the goodwill of a whole array of communities. Notable among these are high school guidance counselors, newspaper columnists, and online bloggers whose comments on the relative merits of particular schools can have a strong influence on the choices people make about where to apply and where to donate.

If EM=C² encompasses not only managing enrollment into student (and other client) communities but also into support, reputational and goodwill communities, it might well be asked: Is there any administrative responsibility that it does not include? Are we merely substituting Enrollment Management for Institutional Management?

We believe that successful enrollment management must evolve beyond the purview of a particular manager, becoming instead more of a discipline that is embraced by all institutional leaders. Consequently, we've broadened the conception of EM beyond student enrollment to include all of the other communities outlined here. The new reality of interconnected communities, social networks and multiple third-party influencers creates both new challenges and new opportunities. Limiting EM's perspective to the flow of students through a funnel limits the institution's ability not only to address challenges but also to seize opportunities.

The impact of an Enrollment Management discipline more broadly conceived than traditionally has been the case, can only be felt when embraced by the many domains comprising the institution. For example:

- EM=C² recognizes that the academic and campus experience is fundamental to shaping the opinions key communities hold about the school and even in determining the effectiveness of recruitment efforts, numbers of applications, and enrolled students. But it does not presume to prescribe changes in academic programming, curricular offerings, pedagogy or other policies affecting faculty. Instead, EM-driven research can offer insights to inform such decisions – but only those who have curricular responsibilities should use these insights to craft their academic offerings.

- Similarly, the C² model recognizes the extent to which an inadequate endowment may critically affect pricing, financial aid policy and the extent of investments in faculty salaries and campus facilities. But decisions regarding fiscal policy and endowment management remain within the purview of other institutional managers. It will be their understanding and support of an effective Enrollment Management discipline that helps to clarify tough trade-off decisions, which in turn will enrich the communities served and the endowments generated.

The EM=C² model can serve as the "C²" example to other institutional domains. If this more expansive, community-focused approach to EM can demonstrate its value to others – faculty leaders, financial and operational managers, even the president and trustees – then it can greatly multiply its impact. C² can introduce the power of community cultivation and leveraging to all sectors of the institution.

––––––––

In the next chapter, we present an EM Matrix that practitioners can use to expand upon the principles of the C² model within their own institutions. Using this matrix, we will explore how thinking in community-centric ways along both the Enrollment and Management axes can help generate fresh insights, practical strategies and a robust EM practice in an increasingly complex and challenging marketplace.

Chapter 5

The EM=C² Matrix

A simple 4x4 matrix can help organize your thinking about how to apply the C² principles of Enrollment Managment.

In the previous chapter, we have described EM=C² as a "complex, adaptive system that is dynamic, nonlinear, emergent and multidimensional." Compared to something as relatively straightforward as the traditional EM model with its sequential phases depicted by that old, (seemingly) reliable funnel metaphor, such a mind-bending reformulation is likely to engender some resistance and not a little eye-rolling. We feel obliged, therefore, to try to cast this new approach within an accessible framework that, at least in spirit, is as elegantly simple as Einstein's original equation.

We tried to think of a real-world metaphor to replace the funnel – synapses in neural networks, interference patterns formed by ripples in a pond, Venn diagrams, or hexagonal icons connecting at intersecting nodes? In the end, we found that a simple 4x4 matrix best captured the interplay between the two fundamental perspectives that have always been central to EM – Enrollment and Management – arrayed respectively along the vertical and horizontal axes.

Before displaying the EM=C² Matrix in all of its elegant simplicity, though, we have a couple of axes to grind. First, we'll take up the E-Axis and then the M-Axis.

The E-Axis: ENROLLMENT

The vertical axis in our matrix is the E-Axis, which stands for the broadened conceptualization of Enrollment that we put forward in Chapter 4: **From the community member's perspective, the process of joining, experiencing, contributing to and transitioning from all kinds of virtual and physical communities.**

Our thinking about what to call the appropriate phases or aspects of the enrollment process has been informed by the literature on the psychology and sociology of community, especially the work of Mc-Millan and Chavis, who are best known for their concept of "Sense of Community" (SOC). They identify four "elements" that, to varying degrees, comprise an individual's SOC.[23]

- ## Membership

  This first element is characterized by boundaries, emotional safety, a sense of belonging and identification, personal investment, and a common symbol system. **In our C² model, Membership includes exploration, inquiry, application to and acceptance into a community.**

- ## Connection

  Termed "shared emotional connection" by McMillan and Chavis, this element depends heavily on participation in – or at least identification with – a shared history. It is strengthened by greater personal interaction (what they call the Contact Hypothesis), quality of interaction, a sense of closure about events, increased perceived importance (valence) of a shared event, greater time and energy invested, more honor (and less humiliation) experienced, and the existence of a spiritual bond. **In our C² model,**

Connection includes interpersonal connection developed in person and electronically.

• Fulfillment

Termed "integration and fulfillment of needs" by McMillan and Chavis, this third element is where "needs" go beyond basic human survival needs to include "that which is desired and valued." Members of groups are seen as being rewarded in various ways for their participation, including the status of being a member, as well as the benefits that might accrue from the competence of other members. **In our C² model, Fulfillment includes the acquisition of knowledge, skills, contacts and other desired benefits of community membership.**

• Influence

This is a bidirectional element. Members of a group must feel empowered to have influence over what a group does and, at the same time, group cohesiveness depends upon the group having some influence over its members. **In our C² model, Influence includes the desire to support and shape the direction of an institution.**

McMillan and Chavis illustrate the dynamics among these four elements with the following example, which happens to be presented in the context of college student life[24].

"Someone puts an announcement on the dormitory bulletin board about the formation of an intramural dormitory basketball team. People attend the organizational meeting as strangers out of their individual needs (integration and **FULFILLMENT** of needs). The team is bound by place of residence (**MEMBER-SHIP** boundaries are set) and spends time together in practice (**CONNECTION** - the Contact Hypothesis). They play a game and win (**CONNECTION** - successful shared valent event). While playing, members exert energy on behalf of the team (**CONNECTION** - personal investment in the group). As the team continues to win, team members become recognized and congratulated (**CONNECTION** - gaining honor and status for being members). Someone suggests that they all buy matching shirts and shoes (**MEMBERSHIP** - common symbols) and they do so (**INFLUENCE**)."

Now, let's translate these four SOC elements into terms a bit more recognizable to Enrollment Managers and others in university administration. Figure 5-1 shows this translation.

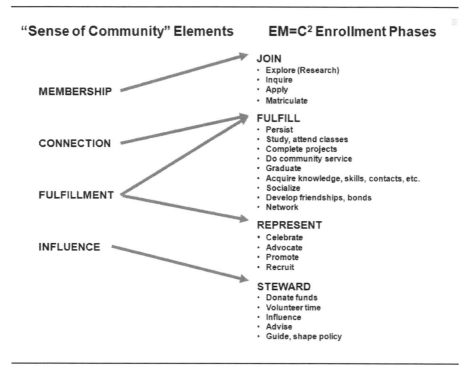

"Sense of Community" Elements   **EM=C² Enrollment Phases**

MEMBERSHIP

CONNECTION

FULFILLMENT

INFLUENCE

JOIN
· Explore (Research)
· Inquire
· Apply
· Matriculate

FULFILL
· Persist
· Study, attend classes
· Complete projects
· Do community service
· Graduate
· Acquire knowledge, skills, contacts, etc.
· Socialize
· Develop friendships, bonds
· Network

REPRESENT
· Celebrate
· Advocate
· Promote
· Recruit

STEWARD
· Donate funds
· Volunteer time
· Influence
· Advise
· Guide, shape policy

Figure 5-1
Relating "Sense of Community" Elements to EM=C² Enrollment Phases

As shown in Figure 5-1, we have grouped an array of activities into four categories that generally match up with the SOC elements, but which also resonate with the types and levels of involvement with institutions of higher education that members of various communities might display. The range of activities highlighted here is not meant to be exhaustive so much as suggestive of what would fall within these broad categories. Let's consider each in turn.

- **JOIN**

   We group under the JOIN phase all of the activities before and including entry into a community. With a student community, for example, these activities include all those associated with the traditional enrollment funnel phases: the exploration of possible college choices (including online research and consultation with third parties), submitting inquiries to the school, applying for admission, and if admitted, agreeing to enroll, confirming enrollment with a deposit, and then actually matriculating. Analogous activities (or relevant subsets of them) would apply to prospective members of other communities, whether they be other client communities or other support, reputational, or goodwill communities. All of them have a JOIN phase during which prospective members with varying degrees of intentionality work their way into an affiliation or relationship with each other and collectively with the institution. Even those who don't complete the JOIN process – those "dark matter" folks who never opt in – continue to be of interest to the institution as potential entrants into the JOIN phase of another community.

- **FULFILL**

   The FULFILL phase encompasses all community member interactions with each other and with the institution in the course of pursuing their goals and satisfying their needs. In keeping with the related SOC elements, those needs can range from the emotional to the social to the pragmatic, as individuals seek to obtain the benefits of being community members. The activities listed in Figure 5-1 are those typically associated with a student community – and more specifically the "retention" phase of the traditional EM paradigm – but expressed here from the student's perspective. Thus, we include persistence in all of its manifestations up to and including obtaining a degree upon graduation. Along the way, students experience the full gamut of what such a community offers to and requires of them – from studying and attending classes to completing assigned projects and participating in extracurricular activities. Socializing and forming friendships that can last a lifetime are all part of the experience. And, as the story of the intramural dormitory basketball team illustrates, there is almost unlimited potential for forming communities within communities.

- ## REPRESENT

  Members of any community might in the course of their experience of that community represent the institution with which it is affiliated – say, as members of a varsity athletic or debate team, or merely wearing a school T-shirt. In our EM=C² model, however, the REPRESENT phase of Enrollment is something more profound. It is a deepening of the relationship between community member and the affiliated institution, such that the member seeks out opportunities to celebrate, advocate on behalf of, promote, and even recruit new members for the institution. In a sense, the individual is moving closer in terms of identification with the school. A person begins as a member of one or more of the institution's many communities and then, by representing the school to others outside of its orbit, he or she begins a process of joining C² – the institution as a Community of Communities.

- ## STEWARD

  We separate out the STEWARD phase of the Enrollment axis because it goes beyond advocacy and other forms of representation to include a substantive commitment of personal time, treasure and/or expertise for the purpose of helping to guide or shape the institution's future direction. This is the "Influence" element of the SOC paradigm made explicit in terms of donating funds, volunteering time, advising academic departments, providing internships, career counseling, hiring graduates, serving as a trustee, safeguarding assets, and shaping institutional policy.

In our expanded definition of Enrollment, all communities, to a greater or lesser extent, can be said to participate in all four of these phases – JOIN, FULFILL, REPRESENT, and STEWARD.

- The student community – the most significant **Client Community** – is, as we've been discussing, heavily invested in the JOIN, FULFILL and REPRESENT dimensions but less so in the STEWARD dimension. Even here, through student government, periodic surveys and Internet chat rooms and blogs, members of a student community can assert considerable influence.

- Alumni donors, on the other hand, as members of a **Support Community**, are more likely to be oriented toward REPRESENT and STEWARD than to JOIN and FULFILL.

- Members of **Reputational and Goodwill Communities** would tend to have even less personal investment in JOIN and FULFILL, as they are less likely to view themselves as distinct communities in relation to the institution. Because they are aware of their power to influence institutional reputation and credibility in the marketplace, however they would be relatively strong in their REPRESENT and STEWARD dimensions.

The M-Axis: MANAGEMENT

Let's turn our attention now to the horizontal axis in our matrix – the M-Axis. This is the broadened notion of Management we described earlier as: **From the institution's perspective, a process of understanding, inspiring, engaging and leveraging all kinds of virtual and physical communities.**

In articulating our understanding of "management" in this context, we've drawn upon our own experience as consultants in the field over several decades. Specifically, we take as our starting point a model we developed at Maguire Associates for assessing institutional capabilities in the realm of strategic planning. We call it the M-SAT

– or Maguire Strategic Aptitude Test – and it measures competency in eight Strategic Aptitudes.[25] They are:

1. **Mission and Values Clarity**
   Widely shared understanding within the institution of its mission, values and distinctive characteristics and competencies. *Understanding who we are.*

2. **Awareness of Key Indicators**
   The ability to identify, track, and continually update the set of key environmental and competitive trends and performance indicators that determine institutional success.
   Recognizing what we need to monitor.

3. **Knowing the Meaning of Information**
   Mastery of the research, analytical, and display techniques that allow for the extraction of meaning and insight from relevant data. *Transforming data into meaningful information.*

4. **Envisioning a Desired Future**
   Engaging periodically in a purposeful exercise of exploring and defining one or more future visions of the institution that fulfill its mission and address challenges and opportunities. *Imagining the kind of institution we want to become.*

5. **Responding to Opportunities and Threats**
   The ability to respond expeditiously to internal and external threats and to take advantage of opportunities as they arise. *Moving with decisiveness and agility in response to unforeseen events.*

6. **Embedding Strategy in Operations**
   The ability to translate broadly defined strategic initiatives into operational terms, thereby assuring implementation and integrating strategic thinking into the ongoing life of the organization. *Making strategy real.*

7. Acting with Alignment

The capacity to follow through on a planned set of actions in a coordinated, coherent way with all relevant parties aligned in a common commitment to achieve the intended results. *Working together toward shared goals.*

8. Learning from Experience

The ability to build upon an evolving knowledge base of what has worked and what has not with each round of strategic thinking, planning, and acting. *Integrating lessons learned to enhance our future success.*

We've purposely chosen to start with a strategic paradigm for the M-Axis because it firmly roots the EM=C² model in the kind of institution-wide, mission-sensitive, competitively aware, and organizationally aligned way of thinking and doing that we believe a strategic approach to management is all about. It certainly is what Enrollment Management's "original synergies" called for. And while we're on that subject, notice that at least three of the eight Strategic Aptitudes – Aptitudes 2, 3 and 8 – have very much to do with metrics and data. This respect for what can be measured and what is meaningful from those measurements undergirds our thinking today every bit as much as it did Jack's over 30 years ago at Boston College.

As with the E-Axis, we've translated these eight dimensions of strategic management into four M-Axis categories that better fit the community-centric nature of our EM=C² model. Figure 5-2 shows the relationship.

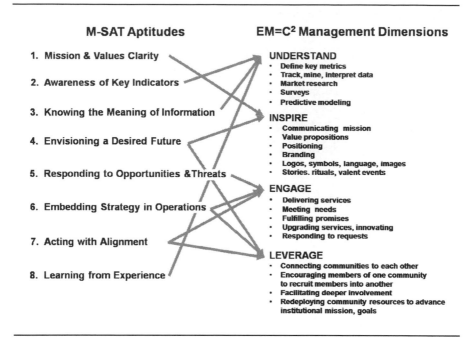

M-SAT Aptitudes

1. Mission & Values Clarity
2. Awareness of Key Indicators
3. Knowing the Meaning of Information
4. Envisioning a Desired Future
5. Responding to Opportunities &Threats
6. Embedding Strategy in Operations
7. Acting with Alignment
8. Learning from Experience

EM=C² Management Dimensions

UNDERSTAND
- Define key metrics
- Track, mine, interpret data
- Market research
- Surveys
- Predictive modeling

INSPIRE
- Communicating mission
- Value propositions
- Positioning
- Branding
- Logos, symbols, language, images
- Stories. rituals, valent events

ENGAGE
- Delivering services
- Meeting needs
- Fulfilling promises
- Upgrading services, innovating
- Responding to requests

LEVERAGE
- Connecting communities to each other
- Encouraging members of one community to recruit members into another
- Facilitating deeper involvement
- Redeploying community resources to advance institutional mission, goals

Figure 5-2
Relating M-SAT Aptitudes to EM=C² Management Dimensions

The institution employs one or more of the following dimensions of Management in seeking to influence the formation and direction of communities.

• UNDERSTAND

The needs, opinions, preferences and actual patterns of inter-action with the institution must be understood to effectively cultivate a community. Toward this end, schools need to define key metrics; track, mine, and interpret data; undertake market research via surveys and focus groups; and employ more so-phisticated techniques such as predictive modeling to gain even greater insight. Understanding communities is not confined to the JOIN phase (of Enrollment) but is an essential management obligation at every phase. The goal at every phase must be to extract the most meaning from the available data as efficiently as possible. In a wired (and increasingly wireless) world awash in data, efficiently extracting meaning may be the biggest challenge of them all.

• INSPIRE

No community forms in relation to an institution without being inspired by some sense of affiliation or identification with its values. $EM=C^2$ is about nurturing that sense of affiliation into ever-deeper commitments to represent, advocate for, support, and ultimately steward the school. To inspire communities, an institution employs a wide array of communications modalities. Fundamental to all of them is the clear articulation of the institution's mission and values. All other elements must align with this "genetic code" of mission and values. The school's specific value propositions, positioning, branding, use of logos, symbols, taglines, images, stories, rituals, and shared events that carry a meaningful emotional charge – all of these elements must be thoughtfully integrated into an inspiring subtext to spark community formation and ongoing commitment.

• ENGAGE

Communities are self-sustaining only to the extent that they are engaged by the institution in ways that produce satisfying experiences and reinforce loyalty. The effectiveness with which the school delivers its basic services (most especially its academic programs) lies at the heart of engagement. Institutional leaders must constantly examine how well the school is meeting the needs of all the communities it serves: students, parents, faculty, alumni, donors, and so many others. How well is the school fulfilling its promises to these communities? At critical "touch points" when students and other constituents make specific requests of the institution, how timely and effective is the response? Is the school missing opportunities to make those experiences positive ones? And, importantly, is the school enhancing the prospects of future engagement by continuously upgrading its services and seeking innovative solutions to past problems?

- ## LEVERAGE

There is a powerful multiplier effect that comes into play when the energies of one community are harnessed on behalf of other communities. Thus, facilitating connections, synergies and transitions between and among communities takes the C^2 paradigm to new levels of impact, as communities leverage one another. Some examples include: connecting one community to another, transitioning members to deeper levels of commitment, and using community resources and outcomes to advance institutional mission and goals more broadly.

The Matrix Reloaded

The matrix that emerges when the E- and M-Axes are combined is displayed in Figure 5-3. Each cell in the matrix defines an E-M intersection that represents a strategic opportunity for community cultivation. This set of C^2 opportunities makes up the basic building blocks of the new EM=C^2 model.

MANAGEMENT

C^2	UNDERSTAND	INSPIRE	ENGAGE	LEVERAGE
JOIN	Understand why and how individuals select and join (or do not) this community.	Inspire individuals to select and join this community.	Engage with individuals as they select and join this community.	Leverage the efforts of individuals as they select and join this community.
FULFILL	Understand why and how members fulfill (or do not) their needs in this community.	Inspire members of this community to more meaningfully fulfill their needs.	Engage members of this community to more effectively fulfill their needs.	Leverage the experience of members of this community as they fulfill their needs.
REPRESENT	Understand why and how members of this community choose to (or not to) represent the school.	Inspire members of this community to represent the school.	Engage members of this community as they represent the school.	Leverage the efforts of members of this community as they represent the school.
STEWARD	Understand why and how members choose to (or not to) steward the school.	Inspire members of this community to steward the school.	Engage members of this community as they steward the school.	Leverage the efforts of members of this community as they steward the school.

(ENROLLMENT axis on left)

Figure 5-3
The EM=C^2 Matrix

The next four chapters will discuss in greater detail each of the four major dimensions of the M-Axis. Chapter 6 explores Understanding Communities; Chapters 7 through 9 discuss Inspiring, Engaging, and Leveraging Communities. Then, in Chapter 10 we demonstrate how various combinations of the 16 Matrix building blocks can be assembled into coherent strategies for addressing some of the more vexing, multi-dimensional challenges facing colleges and universities today.

Chapter 6

Understanding Communities

To understand a community, you gotta love IT!

The first obligation of management with respect to any community is to understand it. That is why we have positioned UNDER-STAND as the first of the four dimensions along the M-Axis. The institutional capacity to understand the needs, preferences, attitudes, opinions and behaviors of communities is essential to inspiring and catalyzing them, engaging and responding to them, and leveraging their influence on other communities.

How is such depth of understanding gained? From a variety of familiar sources, such as: online and hard copy surveys, interviews and focus groups, secondary research of the literature and independent market studies. But more and more, the source of greatest value is the integrated transactional database.

You Gotta Love IT!

As the use of Information Technology infiltrates virtually every aspect of institutional life, advances in transactional databases and reporting make possible the tracking of all manner of contacts (not merely formal transactions) between the institution and all its constituencies (not just students) throughout their lifetimes (not only their campus years.) Without these advanced IT tools, there could be no operationally meaningful C^2 reformulation of Enrollment Management. It would be far too difficult to keep track, much less make sense, of the multiplicity of individual and community interactions.[26]

We are now well past the point where, for most members of higher education communities, immersion in a world mediated by information technology has *become* the community experience. And it can't be dismissed as just the online, virtual stuff. There is a seamlessness now between the "real" world of reunions and alumni maga-

---

Satisfaction with IT Support

Admissions/enrollment officers who are extremely satisfied with their positions report significantly higher satisfaction with their IT support than those who are mostly satisfied or less satisfied with their positions.

	Satisfaction with IT Support*
Extremely Satisfied with Position	3.19
Mostly Satisfied with Position	2.89
Less Satisfied with Position	2.62

Note that none of these groups is very satisfied with IT; all three ratings are near or below the midpoint on the scale.

* Mean Score on a scale of 1-5 where 1 = "Not at all satisfied" and 5 = "Extremely satisfied"

Findings from: Admissions/Enrollment Officers Survey 2008

zines with their class notes on a tangible, printed page and all that real-time, digital *Facebook* messaging. It is now all part of the same IT-mediated, amplified and networked experience. Fortunately for those of us who would seek to understand what this all means, these myriad interactions leave behind a digital data trail. And this data trail contains interpretive information. Thus, IT has become simultaneously the experience and the vehicle for understanding the experience. So whether you like it or not, you gotta love IT.

Not Just Data-Mining . . . Data-Meaning

The number of potential communities of interest and influence is so extensive and the number of potential interactions with those communities so voluminous that any hope of containing operational complexity and cost – not to mention shaping outcomes – depends heavily on a school's capacity to derive meaning from this prodigious data stream.

Use of IT Tools

Enrollment Management is already a technology driven world, as indicated by the following percentages of senior admissions and enrollment officers who actively employ the following electronic / web-based tools in undergraduate recruitment:

Admissions office website	98.0%
Virtual campus tour	56.2
Current student blogs	43.6
Online/web chats	36.7
Instant messaging	35.8
Personalization of the school's website according to prospect preferences	23.0
Text messaging	18.7
Live Webcam from...campus sites	17.1
Podcasts	15.4
Faculty blogs	6.5

Findings from: Admissions/Enrollment Officers Survey 2008

But deriving meaning has always been an iffy proposition, even when it is ostensibly handed to you on a platter – which it rarely is. Cultural anthropologists have long been aware of the dangers of accepting at face value what they are told. For example, there's the story of the anthropologist who visits a "primitive" tribe with the goal of describing what makes it tick. He asks the tribal elders, among other things, where babies come from. Amazingly, they recount a story involving magical animal deities, leaving their visitor to conclude that these poor, benighted folks don't know the first thing about reproductive biology. In actuality, what he was told is the mythology they reserve for outsiders.They know perfectly well how babies are made. They also know how to keep those meddlesome anthropologists guessing.

Every community of interest can be thought of as a tribe. Every institution can be thought of a complex interplay of multiple tribes – a Community of Communities. How do you even begin to make sense of the beliefs and behaviors of any one of those communities, let alone the totality of them? There is certainly value in asking community members what they need, want and intend, but you also need to be very savvy about simply observing what they do.

For example, another kind of cultural anthropology is being practiced by manufacturers of consumer goods. A recent issue of *The New York Times Magazine*[27] featured a Nokia representative whose only job is to travel the world and take hundreds and hundreds of photos of how people use or might use cell phones. The purpose of this unglamorous, on-the-ground intelligence gathering is to help Nokia understand how they can design cell phones that better meet the needs of people in developing countries where the potential for cell phone use is massive. Is it worth it? Well, if Nokia hadn't sent this fellow out there, they wouldn't have found out that because of the monsoon rains, people who live in particular Southeast Asian villages must suspend all household and personal items off the ground lest they be ruined, and Nokia would never have thought to put a hook on the cell phones they plan to market there.

Nokia is by no means alone in using this approach. There are any number of companies acting on this need to better understand the communities they market to, including all those teenage tribes right in their home markets. They identify young people who are hip to the prevailing scene and send them out into those communities to observe and report back on what the kids on the street are actually thinking and doing. Survey, focus group and transactional data are all essential sources of meaning, but they need to be augmented with savvy observation. Sometimes the critical insight is to be found in a single telling quotation, a well-observed anecdote, or a dramatic image in a photograph or video.[28]

Data-meaning, more so than data-mining, requires a willingness to trust the process of letting go of the comforting belief that we already know what we need to know. A true understanding of the lived experience of communities (gained through observation and qualitative insight), combined with quantitative insights (gained through sophisticated analysis of that ever-expanding stream of transactional data), makes for a set of powerful lenses through which to see more meaning-fully how the communities we hope to understand and influence actually think and function.

Social Technographics®

Another powerful tool with which to better understand how people relate to social technologies such as MySpace, Facebook and other online, virtual communities is what Forrester Research calls Social Technographics.[29]

Based on extensive interviews with adults about their attitudes toward and use of these technologies, Forrester identified six "increasing levels of participation" in social technologies. They use the image of a ladder where "participation at one level may or may not overlap with participation at other levels." Starting from the top with the most sophisticated category, the six rungs on the Social Technographics ladder (as described by Forrester) are:

- **Creators**

  "Online [users] who publish blogs, maintain Web pages, or upload videos to sites like YouTube at least once per month. Creators, an elite group, include just 13% of the adult online population." (Note that the category percentages total more than 100 percent, as individuals can participate in multiple categories. For example, 4 out of 10 Creators are Critics as well.)

- **Critics**

  "These online consumers participate in either of two ways - commenting on blogs or posting ratings and reviews on sites like Amazon.com. This level of participation isn't nearly as intense as being a Creator. Critics pick and choose where they want to offer their expertise and often use another blog post or product as the foundation for their contribution. Critics represent 19% of all adult online consumers and on average are several years older than Creators."

- **Collectors**

  "When users save URLs .. [from various sources]..,they create metadata that's shared with the entire community. This act of collecting and aggregating information plays a vital role in organizing the tremendous amount of content being produced by Creators and Critics. Collectors represent 15% of the adult online population."

- **Joiners**

  "This unique group has just one defining behavior – using a social networking site like MySpace.com or Facebook. . . . Joiners represent only 19% of the adult online population and are the youngest of the Social Technographics groups. They are highly likely to engage in other social computing activities."

- **Spectators**

  "This group of blog readers, video viewers, and podcast listeners, which represents 33% of the adult online population, is important as the audience for the social content made by everyone else."

- **Inactives**

  "Today, 52% of online adults do not participate at all in social computing activities."

The above taxonomy of social technology users is useful in at least two ways. First, it helps in developing a more nuanced understanding of how to approach a community that has a significant online presence and has members whose interests and behaviors are understood in the aggregate. Suppose we have a good understanding of the current student community through: a) quantitative analysis of their many transactions with the school as tracked via integrated databases; and b) through qualitative insights based on observation, interviews, focus groups, surveys and the like. What we *don't* have is a good sense of how to access and influence this community in their web-based lives. Knowing that there are potentially six types of online users within this community enables us to seek out the Creators and Critics who wield disproportionate influence within the community. Then we can craft initiatives and messages directed at them that better fit their roles, as distinct from initiatives and messages aimed at Collectors, Joiners, Spectators and Inactives.

In Figure 6-1, we suggest how these same six Social Technographic groups might differ in their degree of investment in the four Enrollment Phases that comprise the E-Axis of the EM=C² Matrix. Where Creators and Critics are likely to evince stronger commitments across all phases, Collectors and Joiners are probably less concerned with REPRESENT and STEWARD than the Creators and Critics, but more so than the Spectators and Inactives. Again, this may prove helpful in crafting more refined strategies and tactical plans for approaching a particular community in its online incarnation.

SOCIAL TECHNOGRAPHIC GROUPS

	CREATORS	CRITICS	COLLECTORS	JOINERS	SPECTATORS	INACTIVES
JOIN	HI	HI	HI	HI	LO	LO
FULFILL	HI	HI	HI	HI	MED	LO
REPRESENT	HI	MED	MED	MED	LO	LO
STEWARD	HI	HI	MED	MED	LO	LO

(Left axis label: ENROLLMENT)

Figure 6-1
E-Axis Enrollment Phases in Relation to Social Technographic Groups

The second way that these Social Technographic categories can be helpful is in thinking of them as potentially applicable to communities in their physical, and not just their online, manifestations. Here we're speaking more conjecturally, as there has been no attempt, as far as we know, to test this hypothesis. However, we can readily imagine individuals who play very similar roles in relation to offline communities. Some alumni, for example, write articles for the alumni magazine or serve on reunion planning committees (Creators), while others hold forth with letters to the editor of the alumni magazine (Critics). Still other alumni serve as class secretaries (Collectors), attendees at class reunions (Joiners), readers of the class notes (Spectators), and as totally uninvolved bystanders (Inactives).

Sharing UNDERSTAND Examples in The Community Square

The "whiteboard" in Figure 6-2 is the first of four (in this and the next three chapters) to capture a few examples of how each of the four M-Axis dimensions – in this case, UNDERSTAND examples – can be applied in practice in relation to various communities and E-Axis phases. By calling these whiteboards "The Community Square," we hope to convey the notion of a public forum where EM practitioners and others may share real-life examples that illustrate the C² approach to Enrollment Management. The Community Square is alive online at the URL shown on page 133. We invite you to join the conversation already in progress.

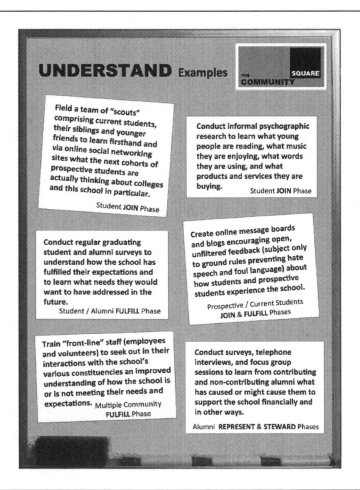

Figure 6-2
The Community Square UNDERSTAND Examples

Understanding communities, as we've suggested, is fundamental to any well-conceived EM effort aimed at addressing community needs and interests or influencing community attitudes and behaviors. In the next chapter we discuss how Inspiring communities can build on this understanding, but only after the institution has done the hard work of understanding itself – what it stands for and why.

Chapter 7

Inspiring Communities

Like the genetic code in the nucleus of the cell, an institution's mission and values are at the core of every community and the connections between them.

Communities that form in relation to an institution are at some level inspired by a sense of affiliation or identification with it. Members of such communities need not hold the same opinions about the school, but they share a common bond. That bond may be as ephemeral as an interest in learning more about the school in the course of a college search process. Or it may be strong and durable, as in the case of alumni who maintain affiliation over their lifetimes. Mere awareness of the institution does not a community make.

To Inspire Is to DNAble

Used in this context, "inspiring" means articulating, burnishing and disseminating a set of core ideas – the school's DNA of Values – that can catalyze the formation of a community or help assure its continuation. The uplifting sense of "inspire" is not without relevance, though, as a tarnished or compromised set of core values can have devastating consequences for the formation and maintenance of communities that would share any sense of affiliation with the institution.

The DNA of core values resides within the institution's "brand" – an aura of associations that may have built up in a person's consciousness over years via the media and periodic contact. Or, the DNA may have indelibly left its mark on (branded?) someone through intense personal involvement (for example, during a student's undergraduate years). Whether viewed as a clearly defined set of ideas or as a more nebulous image, this sense of what a particular school stands for and what distinguishes it from other schools lies at the heart of community, even if it is not constantly referenced by each of its members.

This sense is also what helps connect one community to another (as you'll see in the Chapter 9 discussion of Leveraging). In an organ transplant, the closer the DNA match between the donor and the recipient, the more likely the organ will not be rejected. We see a similar phenomenon in the recruiting of prospective students. The chances of a good match between student and school are greatly enhanced when there is a shared set of values. The school that knows its own DNA can better search for and identify prospective students, donors and others who resonate with and are attracted to it.

Embrace Thy Genome!
The Delphic Oracle's admonition: "Know thyself!" is an essential first step in Inspiring communities. To continue the DNA metaphor we might rephrase it: "Embrace thy genome!"

The pressures exerted upon schools by college rankers to conform to their all-powerful standards (as described in Chapter 2), coupled with the financial pressures to maximize revenues can all too easily persuade institutional leaders to compromise their DNA of core values, or, at a minimum, to modify the brand. At some point, these compromises and modifications will so muddy an institution's image and garble its message that the resulting confusion can lead to a kind of cognitive dissonance (internally as well as externally). As a consequence, key prospect or influence communities fail to take root, or wither and die.

Over the years, we have far more often advised institutional leaders to embrace what is most authentic about their school and seek out students for whom it has genuine appeal, than we have encouraged them to change their institutional DNA in ways that will make their school more appealing to a broader, less discriminating public. There are certainly exceptions, as when core values are way out of synch with the times – one example is historically exclusionary schools that need to be more open to a diverse student mix. But even then, it can be important to tap into the institution's historical legacy for recognizable themes that are truly distinctive.

The Mission/Values Challenge

Three Enrollment Officers comment on what they see as the "most important problem facing college admissions today."

"Institutions responding to rating, for they often contradict the mission and vision of the institution by forcing the institution to make decisions that promote marketing over substance."

"Too many colleges are trying to brand themselves, remake themselves, push their profiles, etc. – rather than developing the best possible programs and services for the students who naturally choose the institution."

"Ensuring that we maintain ethical standards and stay focused on what's good for students at a time when competition and pressure are fierce."

Comments from: Admissions/Enrollment Officers Survey 2008

Every institution has the power to define itself specifically and uniquely in terms of what distinguishes it from other institutions – what values it holds most dear, what it seeks to achieve on behalf of its students, how it goes about teaching, and what kinds of students it hopes to serve – in short, its institutional DNA. Armed with this self-knowledge and sophisticated research and analytical tools, schools can now identify with much greater precision the prospects most likely to apply and enroll. The result is that schools don't have to compromise their principles to gather an entering class.

The critical tasks of identifying, articulating and disseminating a school's core values and distinguishing features can involve a whole arsenal of tools and techniques: mission statements, logos, mottos, taglines, color schemes, mascots, signage, letterhead, collateral materials, website design, etc. Whatever the combination of design elements and media, it all comes down to assembling words and images that convey the essence of an institution's values and identity. Editorial and graphic design skill can take a set of solid core ideas and do wonders to make them compelling and evocative. But no amount of design magic can transform core ideas that are inauthentic, imitative or merely opportunistic into a truly effective catalyst for community formation or a cohesive bond that reinforces community persistence.

There is no shortcut to inspiring communities. It requires the hard work of defining "who we are." And, while a Mission Statement may be one output of this effort, the crafting of such a statement, if made the primary focus, can so easily devolve into a wordsmithing exercise by committee as to yield merely the most generically lofty and least offensive expression of institutional purpose, coming nowhere close to capturing what is truly distinctive about the school. The work of self-discovery may take many meetings involving the governing board, senior administration and faculty leadership, and extensive feedback from students, alumni and other communities before a school arrives at a meaningful synthesis. Or, it may happen relatively quickly and with little fanfare. We have witnessed and, on occasion facilitated, numerous institutional efforts to do this important work. We have seen it play out both in agonizingly slow fashion, as contending camps battle over the "soul" of the school, and expeditiously with little acrimony and much celebration. When this kind of introspective institutional soul-searching comes easily with broad concurrence, there is a much greater chance that the school has the kind of substrate of self-knowledge upon which a commitment to community building can thrive.

Sharing INSPIRE Examples in the Community Square

In Figure 7-1 we post six examples of how institutions are already Inspiring communities. What are some examples from your experience? See page 133 for the online address of The Community Square and let us know.

Figure 7-1
The Community Square INSPIRE Examples

———

Understanding and Inspiring communities will typically lead to Engaging them. But engagement that's merely reactive and perfunctory offers little prospect for positive, enduring outcomes in terms of enhancing any of the phases of Enrollment from JOIN to STEWARD. By contrast, engagement that is smart, proactive and beneficial to all parties requires careful thought and disciplined execution. More about this in the next chapter.

Chapter 8

Engaging Communities

Once inspired to form, a community will survive only as long as its engagement with the school continues to reinforce the sense of identification or affiliation of its various members.

The fact of community quickly gives way to the experience of community, which is the sum total of all of the members' many individual interactions with the institution over time. Some of these interactions are transactional (a student registering for a course or paying a bill at the bursar's office) and many others are informational or assistive (e.g., an inquirer requesting a packet of material about a particular program through the school's website or an alumnus seeking news about job opportunities via an online alumni database). All these interactions, and so many more, are the stuff of community engagement. Not surprisingly, some interactions hold greater potential for community building than others. The surprise is which ones.

Problematic Opportunities
When it comes to more effectively engaging all kinds of communities, especially Student/Client and Support Communities, colleges

and universities can learn much from the field of Customer Relationship Management (CRM[30]), which has become one of the most broadly accepted "best practice" disciplines in business management. A big lesson of customer loyalty programs and CRM generally is that the most satisfied customers are often those who have experienced a problem that has been positively resolved. CRM, in other words, is not so much about the impossible goal of preventing all problems that might produce a dissatisfied customer as it is about being so on top of the problems that do occur that the problem resolution experience actually leaves the customer more satisfied than he/she was in the first place. That's because any time you have a chance for a meaningful interaction of any sort, there is an opportunity to strengthen the customer relationship.

Telephone fundraisers approach their work in a similar spirit, turning what is usually experienced as an intrusion into a problem-solving opportunity. In what is perhaps the most extreme example of a concentrated, intrusive "sales" interaction, the fundraiser has barely a minute or two to make a personal connection with a potential donor – who very likely was interrupted doing something far more enjoyable, like having dinner. The most successful callers are certainly well-spoken and passionate about their cause, but they are also trained to welcome objections. Why? Because the objection keeps the conversation going. The objection is the best evidence of an engaged potential donor. Armed with all possible objections (and their most effective responses), the caller is prepared to solve the donor's problem.

Problems are opportunities – whether on the telephone seeking a donation, on the Internet responding to an applicant's concern, or in an office on campus addressing a student's most perplexing dilemma. But the key to transforming all these problematical touch points into positive experiences is to attract, hire, train, recognize and reward the people who "get" what it means to be a facilitator of the experience – a steward of the institutional brand.

The most successful companies have adopted a somewhat counterintuitive philosophy. Instead of arming their senior executives and middle managers with these special interaction skills, they arm the front-line troops who are the ones most likely to be engaged in these kinds of customer interactions and who typically have been the most underprepared.

Higher education, on the whole, is only beginning to come to grips with the fact that students and their parents, donors, volunteers and any number of other communities are "customers." Many schools are probably years away from hiring, training and rewarding people in the bursar's office, the registrar's office, and the financial aid office who actually think in terms of customer loyalty or Customer Relationship Management. Why is that?

Part of the reason may be that few college and university presidents think of themselves as guardians and facilitators of community experiences – as leaders who themselves need to model the same engagement behaviors as those serving on the front lines. If presidents don't recognize that administrative staff and faculty are also part of the experience, it's very unlikely that the chief financial officer, the enrollment manager, the financial aid director, the provost or the professor and all others on down the line will embrace this philosophy either.

Troubling "SatisFictions"

The high cost of a college education has shifted the cost-benefit calculus of enrolled students such that they are more willing to transfer to another school if their academic and campus life expectations have not been met. Competition for students (including transfer students) has so intensified as to give such disaffected students plenty of options. On the principle that your most valuable (and least costly to acquire) "customers" are those you already have, efforts to retain them through graduation – and beyond, as alumni supporters, donors, and parents of future students – become essential components of any lifespan approach to Enrollment Management. Thus, "student engagement" has emerged as an increasingly popular theme, especially as it impacts student retention.

A useful tool for thinking about what happens in the minds of students during the retention phase is the Satisfaction-Retention Matrix (Figure 8-1).

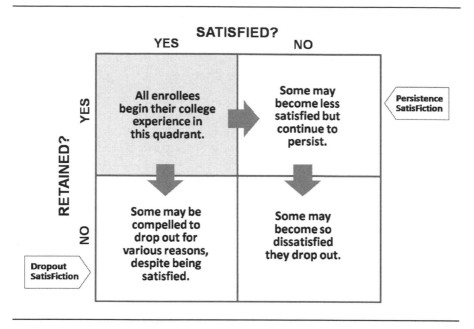

SATISFIED?

YES   NO

All enrollees begin their college experience in this quadrant.

Some may become less satisfied but continue to persist.

Persistence SatisFiction

Some may be compelled to drop out for various reasons, despite being satisfied.

Some may become so dissatisfied they drop out.

Dropout SatisFiction

RETAINED? YES / NO

Figure 8-1
Satisfaction — Retention Matrix

- All enrollees begin their college experience in the upper left quadrant. They are both satisfied and retained. Over time, some may become less satisfied yet continue to persist (upper right.) As time goes on and they (and their parents) are increasingly invested in the school and accrued credits may be prove increasingly difficult to transfer to another institution, their dissatisfaction may be overridden by a willingness to persist through degree completion. Chances are these graduates will not become major supporters of their Alma Mater as alumni.

- Some, however, may become so dissatisfied they drop out (lower right.) And there are others who, although satisfied, are compelled to leave for academic, personal and/or financial reasons (lower left.)

• There are likely to be some students for whom this school was not their first choice. They may move quickly into the upper right quadrant, where they are at risk of dropping out early. If they cannot be retained, they may need help in finding a more suitable school.

The institution's objective should be to maximize the number of enrollees in the upper left quadrant over the full extent of their academic careers, retaining them with a high degree of satisfaction through graduation.

Notice we've labeled the upper right quadrant "Persistence Satis-Fiction" and the lower left quadrant "Dropout SatisFiction." We call them Satis*Fictions* because in both cases the students involved are making decisions which belie their ostensible satisfaction levels – decisions that are suboptimal and potentially damaging to the school. We strongly urge any student engagement strategy to target these two "SatisFiction" categories.

• Persistence SatisFiction

Students who persist at a school despite relatively low levels of satisfaction are not only at risk of becoming less than supportive alumni, but may also actually be proactive in spreading their negative opinions of the institution. Should they do so via the Internet with all its potential for viral amplification, the damage to the school's reputation and future recruitment efforts could be substantial. To forestall such an outcome, the school would do well to continually monitor student satisfaction levels and take steps that improve those levels, especially on behalf of students in this category. Should such efforts fail, follow-up actions to mitigate the consequences of their disaffection would certainly be in order. Some schools, for example, continue to extend the career enhancement benefits of being part of its extended network of former students, whether or not they have completed their studies.

Retaining the Underprepared

In our 2006 Chronicle survey, college faculty members expressed concern about the inadequate preparation of entering freshmen for college level work.[31] One faculty member offered this trenchant analysis.

"Part of the problem of inadequate preparation is structural. Shifts in labor markets, the transformation of the campus into a rite of passage for middle class kids, and the corresponding inflation of academic degrees, have meant many more young people are in college now that might not have been there a generation ago. On top of that, colleges have become more entrepreneurial. In competition with each other, institutions of higher education have become more consumer-friendly, and in somecases—perhaps many—that means lowering academic standards."

Comments from: Teachers and Faculty Survey 2006

• **Dropout SatisFiction**

Students who drop out despite relatively high levels of satisfaction are not only depriving the school of potentially high-performing, satisfied students and alumni, but also of potential long-term supporters whose value to the school could include all the Enrollment phases of the EM=C² Matrix after JOIN—from FULFILL to REPRESENT to STEWARD. With appropriate support, members of this group might be retained – if not as current students, then as future recipients of service or as future donors. Some in this quadrant may leave only because their career objectives have changed and the school no longer meets their needs, although they continue to hold the school in high regard. Helping them transfer to a more appropriate setting may be rewarded by the maintenance of a long-term relationship that includes adult education, financial support and/or future student referrals.

As it happens, the Satisfaction-Retention Matrix is relevant to every Enrollment (E-Axis) phase of every community affiliated with the school, and the logic in each case is similar. There is a degree of member satisfaction and a decision – to persist or to drop out of that community or persist in one phase of community membership without moving on to a phase of deeper commitment. An example would be an alumnus who maintains a continuing FULFILL status, enjoying the benefits of alumni networking and programming with no interest in assuming REPRESENT or STEWARD roles. A school can develop individualized Engagement strategies based on where among the four quadrants a particular community member is positioned.

The Era of Relativity

We take our fascination with Dr. Einstein yet another step by suggesting that there is indeed a fourth dimension to community engagement – time. And, it will come as no surprise that in this context, time is very relative indeed. It may even slow down as you approach the speed of Community!

Think of it this way. Communities exist over time, requiring that we engage them in time-sensitive ways that deepen their connection with the institution and with each other. Cultivating and maintaining alumni communities, for example, thus becomes an exercise in era-specific communications. Each cohort of alumni can be addressed as they were, as they are, and as they might become in relation to the school. This same phenomenon also applies to communities of parents, donors, faculty, staff and others whose experience with the institution has been shaped by a particular era.

Here are a few examples of the relativity of the time dimension when it comes to engaging and connecting different cohorts of student and alumni communities:

- Engaging alumni who are nostalgic for their student days can keep them forever young and connected with the school that they remember.

- Communicating with alumni about the school as it is today can keep them forever young at heart, as they continue to see the school through the eyes of its current students.

- Reminding alumni of eras before their own helps connect them to the school's core mission and values that had persisted into their time and will persist into the future.

- Connecting today's students with alumni keeps the school's heritage alive and deepens their own connections with school as they become alumni.

Sharing ENGAGE Examples in The Community Square

Once again, we post several examples of how this important M-Axis dimension can be expressed in in real-life, operational terms. See Figure 8-2.

————

In a sense, any and all activities that involve interacting with community members are acts of engagement. But there are some worth distinguishing from others. These are the initiatives undertaken to LEVERAGE efforts of the members of one community on behalf of the members of another community. The next chapter treats this next level of EM effectiveness.

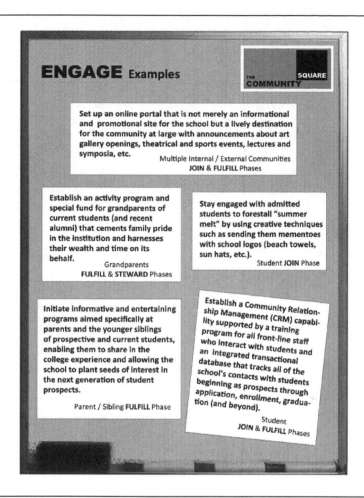

ENGAGE Examples

COMMUNITY SQUARE

Set up an online portal that is not merely an informational and promotional site for the school but a lively destination for the community at large with announcements about art gallery openings, theatrical and sports events, lectures and symposia, etc.

Multiple Internal / External Communities
JOIN & FULFILL Phases

Establish an activity program and special fund for grandparents of current students (and recent alumni) that cements family pride in the institution and harnesses their wealth and time on its behalf.

Grandparents
FULFILL & STEWARD Phases

Stay engaged with admitted students to forestall "summer melt" by using creative techniques such as sending them mementoes with school logos (beach towels, sun hats, etc.).

Student **JOIN** Phase

Initiate informative and entertaining programs aimed specifically at parents and the younger siblings of prospective and current students, enabling them to share in the college experience and allowing the school to plant seeds of interest in the next generation of student prospects.

Parent / Sibling **FULFILL** Phase

Establish a Community Relationship Management (CRM) capability supported by a training program for all front-line staff who interact with students and an integrated transactional database that tracks all of the school's contacts with students beginning as prospects through application, enrollment, graduation (and beyond).

Student
JOIN & FULFILL Phases

Figure 8-2
The Community Square ENGAGE Examples

Chapter 9

Leveraging Communities

Connections, transitions, and facilitations between communities take the C² model to new levels of impact.

There is a powerful multiplier effect that comes into play when the energies of one community are harnessed on behalf of another community. So much so, that the ultimate benefits of the C² model of Enrollment Management are most fully realized when communities are encouraged to connect with, support and leverage one another.

The Meaningfulcrum

To get a sense of the leveraging potential of communities, visualize pairs of communities on two ends of a lever with a fulcrum closer to one end than the other (as in Figure 9-1). A relatively small force applied by Community A on the long end can exert a greater force on Community B on the short end.

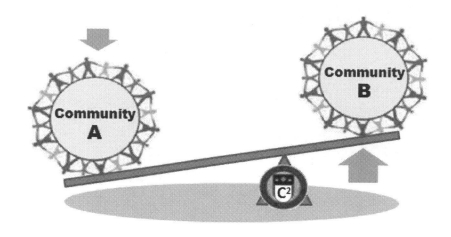

Figure 9-1
Community A Leveraging Community B

Now, think of the fulcrum as the institutional mission and values (or brand) we described in Chapter 6: Inspiring Communities. The closer this "meaningfulcrum" is to Community B, the more effective will be the leveraging efforts of Community A. Or, to put it less metaphorically, the institutional brand can be powerfully moving, if it is meaningfully close to the hearts and minds of those whose support is being sought. It is this set of shared institutional values that enables one affiliated community to positively affect the experiences and behaviors of another.

Leveraging Options

Let's now depict these two communities (A and B) in relation to each other by representing one on a vertical E-Axis and the other on a horizontal E-Axis (as shown in both parts of Figure 9-2).

In the first case, we see Community A leverage Community B; and in the second, Community B leverage Community A. In both cases, the leveraging options are the same but complementary. When those in the same Enrollment phase of their respective communities interact, they Reinforce each other's experience (the diagonal cells).

Community A Leveraging Community B

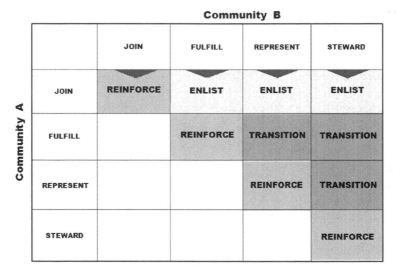

Community B

	JOIN	FULFILL	REPRESENT	STEWARD
JOIN	REINFORCE			
FULFILL	ENLIST	REINFORCE		
REPRESENT	ENLIST	TRANSITION	REINFORCE	
STEWARD	ENLIST	TRANSITION	TRANSITION	REINFORCE

Community A

Community B Leveraging Community A

Community B

	JOIN	FULFILL	REPRESENT	STEWARD
JOIN	REINFORCE	ENLIST	ENLIST	ENLIST
FULFILL		REINFORCE	TRANSITION	TRANSITION
REPRESENT			REINFORCE	TRANSITION
STEWARD				REINFORCE

Community A

Figure 9-2
Community Leveraging Options

When those who have moved beyond the JOIN phase of the leveraging community interact with those who are still in the JOIN phase of the other community, they can Enlist (or recruit) them to JOIN. And when those in the REPRESENT or STEWARD phases of the leveraging community interact with those in earlier phases of the other community, they can Transition them to the next deeper phase of Enrollment commitment – from FULFILL to REPRESENT and from REPRESENT to STEWARD.

How do these three kinds of Leveraging – to Reinforce, Enlist, and Transition – actually play out in the lives of communities? Below, we offer some examples.

• Leveraging to Reinforce

In theory, any satisfied member of one community can reinforce the positive experiences of members of another. But when the parties involved are in similar phases of their respective communities, an especially promising opportunity presents itself for them to mutually reinforce their experience of that phase. We see it when donors from one college class solicit donations from those in another class. And we see it when upperclassmen (and women) reach out to assist students who are in an earlier stage of their academic careers.

• Leveraging to Enlist

This form of leveraging has a long history in higher education. We see it whenever folks from one group are involved in recruiting folks from another – enlisting them into the ranks of students, donors, volunteers, etc. Alumni have long been an important source of student recruitment support. In Chapter 1 we described how 30 years ago Boston College was already involving alumni in the student recruitment effort.[32] And students can be particularly effective fundraisers, reaching out to alumni who shared similar interests, such as Glee Club, sports teams, and majors.

- ## Leveraging to Transition

  When members of one community have "walked the walk" by deepening their own personal commitments to the institution (or as we would say in our model, Transitioning from FULFILL to REPRESENT or STEWARD), they are especially persuasive in facilitating deeper commitments by members of other communities. Again, the alumni become a valued resource for this type of leveraging, but members of any community who have progressed to more committed phases can help to Transition others both within their own and in other communities.

We Never Meta-Lever We Didn't Like

We can't leave the topic of community leveraging without speaking of what we might call "meta-leveraging." This would include all the ways that the institution as a Community of Communities can take advantage of lessons learned and/or resources generated from particular communities. Meta-leveraging goes beyond what members of one community might do to Reinforce, Enlist or Transition members of another community to what the institution as a whole might do to benefit more broadly from the experience of individual communities. There are at least two ways meta-leveraging can work: Replication and Redeployment.

- ## Meta-leveraging to Replicate

  In our Chapter 5 discussion of M-Axis dimensions, we referred to the Strategic Aptitude of "Learning from Experience" (defined as: "integrating lessons learned to enhance…future success"). In furtherance of this aptitude, an institution seeking to build on its past success in nurturing a new community to form and evolve will want to replicate that experience in other settings. Each cohort of alumni volunteers, for example, whose efforts Reinforce and Transition the experiences of their classmates is itself a replicable community. Each group of journalists, commentators, and higher education opinion leaders in a given regional market is yet another replicable community. In these and similar instances, the institution is leveraging by replication the lessons learned at a higher, meta level.

- **Meta-Leveraging to Redeploy**

  Another type of meta-leveraging is the redeployment of resources generated through community cultivation to fuel other strategically valid institutional initiatives. A good example of this is applying the fundraising proceeds garnered from the STEWARD phase of an alumni community to the funding of financial aid on behalf of the JOIN phase of a prospective student (Applicant) community. Meta-leveraging to redeploy resources tends to involve fungible resources like contributed dollars more than human resources, as the latter more appropriately fit the basic leveraging model discussed earlier.

Sharing LEVERAGE Examples in The Community Square

Figure 9-3 is the LEVERAGE space in The Community Square where we post some noteworthy examples of the four M-Axis dimensions. We hope you will too, at the web site shown on page 133.

———

In this and the preceding three chapters, we've explored some of the more pertinent factors affecting the Management of Enrollment – the M-Axis of our EM=C² Matrix. Along the way, we highlighted examples of how the four Management dimensions of UNDERSTAND, INSPIRE, ENGAGE, and LEVERAGE find expression in colleges and universities today.

In the five chapters that follow, we try to paint a more complete and true-to-life picture of EM=C² in action. We revisit the five challenging scenarios sketched out at the beginning of this book and fill in more of the brushstrokes, describing how, by using C² principles, the protagonists in those painful episodes respond constructively to the dilemmas they face and turn them into Challenging Opportunities.

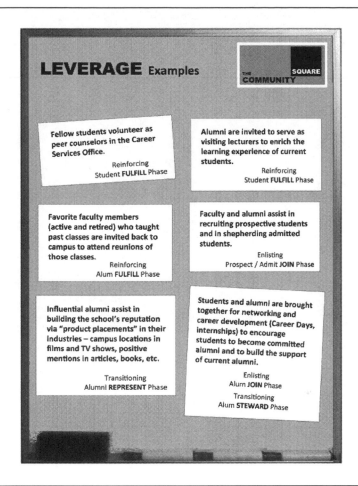

LEVERAGE Examples

THE COMMUNITY SQUARE

Fellow students volunteer as peer counselors in the Career Services Office.
Reinforcing
Student **FULFILL** Phase

Alumni are invited to serve as visiting lecturers to enrich the learning experience of current students.
Reinforcing
Student **FULFILL** Phase

Favorite faculty members (active and retired) who taught past classes are invited back to campus to attend reunions of those classes.
Reinforcing
Alum **FULFILL** Phase

Faculty and alumni assist in recruiting prospective students and in shepherding admitted students.
Enlisting
Prospect / Admit **JOIN** Phase

Influential alumni assist in building the school's reputation via "product placements" in their industries – campus locations in films and TV shows, positive mentions in articles, books, etc.
Transitioning
Alumni **REPRESENT** Phase

Students and alumni are brought together for networking and career development (Career Days, internships) to encourage students to become committed alumni and to build the support of current alumni.
Enlisting
Alum **JOIN** Phase
Transitioning
Alum **STEWARD** Phase

Figure 9-3
The Community Square LEVERAGE Examples

Chapter 10

Five Challenging Opportunities

Starting with this chapter, we revisit the troubling case studies with which we began this book. Here we develop these scenarios in greater detail and, in doing so, show how the more expansive conception of Enrollment Management we propose could hold the keys to addressing these difficult issues successfully. Before we begin with the first of these cases, a note about how they are written and how they are presented.

How Written

Our Maguire Associates colleagues contributed to all aspects of this book, and we very much appreciate their insights and creativity throughout. This is particularly true in these next five chapters, where we asked colleagues to develop case studies in light of their own experience in consulting to clients facing similar issues. We also encouraged them to combine client experiences if necessary to make a point, and to use a bit of poetic license in describing initiatives that may not have actually been taken but which, in their professional judgment, they would propose be taken.

How Presented

Closing the loop on our presentation of the EM=C² paradigm, we present these case discussions with enough comparability that you will readily see how they connect with the Matrix and, hence, with the C² principles. We figured the least intrusive way to do this is through the use of icons referencing the two axes of the Matrix.

Management		Enrollment	
UNDERSTAND	🔍	🗝	JOIN
INSPIRE	🔥	📜	FULFILL
ENGAGE	☞	🚩	REPRESENT
LEVERAGE	⚖	⚱	STEWARD

Note that we place the M-icons before the E-icons and indicate a direction from M to E. This is because the initiatives referenced in these five case studies all concern institutional actors Managing Enrollment. There are 16 combinations of M and E-Icons, and these various pairings will, as appropriate, appear to the left of the relevant initiative, action, or concept presented in the text.[33]

Stealth Applicants

The Invasion of the Invisible Inquirers

The EM Challenge

Virginia Rhodes was biting her fingernails on a cold January morning, a few days after Thoreau University's admissions application deadline. She was at a loss. Her Admissions Director had just given her a report that showed a fourth consecutive year of increasing "stealth applicants." As VP of Enrollment Management, Virginia had been growing more concerned over the past few years about "stealth applicants," prospective students for whom the application itself is the very first tangible contact with the institution. They've gone from comprising 15 percent of the total application pool just three years ago up to 25 percent, then to 33 percent last year, and *a full 40 percent today.*

Now, these invisible applicants comprised almost half of her applicant pool. "Who *are* these students?" she wondered. "Where do they come from and who influenced them to apply? Was it just the website? Or was it something or someone else? How can we know more? And why are there so many prospective students who don't want us to know about them in advance? If I were a high school student, I'd love to get our brochures and viewbook in the mail and be invited to all the recruitment events. We offer so much!"

She felt as though she had lost control of Thoreau U's recruitment funnel, and that was extremely disconcerting. Just a few years back, she could clearly chart the progression from prospects to applicants. Virginia could accurately project the application numbers early in the cycle based on the number of inquirers. There was a comfort in the *inevitability* of the annual recruitment cycle, from the name buys and search outreach to the paper application mailing in late August. But now, it seemed, there was no way to know that or to do much about it. The projections came out frighteningly low because so many students never even inquired for more information.

Virginia sighed and blew on her coffee. She had already begun to wonder whether the costly search and recruitment rigmarole was worth all the effort and rising expense if prospective students were just going to lurk invisibly in cyberspace waiting to apply anyway. Clearly, student behaviors had shifted and were continuing to change, while TU's strategies and tactics remained the same.

In this environment, she wondered how she could effectively manage recruitment and enrollment of the class when she didn't know a thing about 40 percent of her applicants until very late in the game. A nervous feeling spread through her stomach. "What happens if next year there are even more stealth applications? Or worse, what happens if next year there aren't *any*?" There seemed to be no way to know. The elephant in the room was the question of what it all meant for Thoreau U's enrollment, not just for one year but also the long term. She felt as if she might as well throw her projections right out the window. Unless her President, Dr. Benjamin Plutarch, threw her out the window first. She tapped her pen on the desk, bit another fingernail, sipped some coffee, and asked, "Who *are* these students?"

The C² Opportunities

This "stealth application" scenario represents a challenge being faced or soon to be faced by many experienced enrollment professionals. The dynamics of student recruitment continue to change in the digital and wireless world that high school students inhabit. The paradigm of predictability – large name buys lead to large inquirer pools lead to large applicant pools – that offered so much success in the 1990s now requires sophisticated analytical thinking and research efforts to ensure that recruitment initiatives are being optimized and that limited financial resources are being deployed on efforts that produce verifiable success.

Look Back

  One of the first steps that Virginia Rhodes could take is to gather as much information as possible about the current and previous years' stealth applicants. In order to begin to understand how and why students join the "stealth application" community, she could first learn about who they are. It's unfortunate that many EM professionals mistakenly view deep explorative research as a luxury undertaken only when there's extra time and money. In fact, probative research is needed most in precisely the opposite scenario: when there's no time and there are pressing budgetary issues.

Thoreau U must identify characteristics of the stealth applicants and compare those students to the more traditional applicant who inquired and communicated with the institution before applying. Where are the stealth applicants from? Is that different than the rest of the applicant pool? How admissible are the students? Of those who are admitted, what percentage tend to enroll? Is that "yield" better or worse than other admitted students? Any and all information that might distinguish the "stealthy" audience from the one traditionally served by TU could lead to an ability to better influence those students to make themselves known.

Look Up

It's also important to climb back up the conventional admissions funnel and see if any of those "stealthy" students were actually part of any Search name buys back at the very beginning of the recruitment process. If they were and chose not to respond to Thoreau's outreach efforts, but still applied, what was missing in the message that led those prospects to pass up the opportunity to engage earlier? If any of the previous years' stealth applicants enrolled (or if current year stealth applicants would like to participate by phone), the university could convene focus groups to discuss these very issues.

There are a variety of ways to extract golden nuggets of information that are essential to understanding the experience of a stealth applicant. What if they tell you that it was simply too much of a hassle to locate the inquiry form on the website? What if the form was too long and cumbersome and many just didn't want to bother? In these cases, the institution could make technical and procedural adjustments to make inquiring more accessible and simpler. It's also quite common that students simply aren't being told what's in it for *them* if they fill out an online inquiry form. In that case, Thoreau can enhance the messaging to explain why it will benefit the student to be on the mailing list. Sometimes, when you want to know something from an audience, the best thing to do is just to *ask them.*

Look Underneath

If the university can learn who influences these prospective students and how, they might be able to take action with those influencing communities. For example, if the major influence is, in fact, the institutional website, Thoreau might decide to invest in making a more interactive and dynamic website that allows truly useful personalization if the visitor simply shares a few pieces of key information, including their interests and contact information. On some admissions sites, the staid old "Inquirer Form" is not only unwieldy, but promises little in the way of direct value to the prospective student. Instead of framing the interaction as one that provides the university with the student's information, the interaction can instead give prospective students direct and fluid access to the multimedia information they most desire in exchange for some personal information.

  Or, if it turns out that guidance counselors wield the most direct influence on stealth applicants, a proactive effort to reach out through phone calls, electronic newsletters, and other means to the vast guidance counselor community might be in order. Again, if a school wants these influential guidance counselors to encourage their students to sign in and make themselves known, it can reach out to make the case that this is good for the students and good for the counselor! If Thoreau U can understand how stealth applicants experience their college search process through some of these survey and focus group methods, they take a giant leap forward towards developing ideas and strategies that inspire these students to join the inquirer community, thus giving the University more opportunity to engage them directly.

  This type of digging beneath the surface, once thought to yield almost no useful information, can uncover a world of opportunity to leverage the communities that actively influence the "stealth application" population and encourage them to change course. After all, if stealth applicants comprise 40 percent of the applicant pool, isn't it essential to try to reach the countless additional "stealth inquirers" to whom the school would welcome communicating its distinctive message more proactively?

Look Inside

Quite frequently, stealth applicants yield from admitted student to enrolling student at lower rates than the more traditional applicants. It's hard to say whether that's because they are simply an audience destined to have lower levels of interest or because they just haven't had the time or amount of contact to learn all about the wonderful experiences and education each institution offers. If this is true for Thoreau U, there are a variety of options described above for engaging a seemingly invisible audience earlier in the process. But, what about those who have arrived this year as stealth applicants and those who inevitably will in the future, the best and most strategic recruitment initiatives notwithstanding?

The goal is to enhance the stealth applicant's experience once the application is submitted in an effort to inspire and engage them to join the enrolled student experience. There are active communities that someone like Virginia Rhodes can leverage to help meet that objective. At Thoreau, there are vibrant com-

munities of alumni active in recruiting new students. There is also a vibrant community of current students excited to do the same. These groups can participate, both on campus and out in the prospective students' home communities, in promoting Thoreau to the stealth applicants – and to other applicants as well.

A lesser-utilized community available to Thoreau, and any other institution that offers a binding early decision application and enrollment option, are those students already admitted and committed to enroll with TU as their undisputed first-choice institution. These students are often the least intimidating of any recruitment community, as they are nearly always in the exact same educational situation: about to enroll in the first year of college for the very first time. Unlike older alumni and current students who can be several years the stealth applicant's senior, Early Decision students are on the same level, are prospective classmates of the stealth applicants, and are nearly always and enthusiastic about their new university community.

Conclusion

At her desk nearly a year later, Virginia Rhodes calmly sipped her coffee on a cold December morning, just weeks before the upcoming application deadline. She was careful not to chip her beautifully manicured fingernails that shined in Thoreau's colors, not a tooth mark upon them. After committing herself to understanding the stealth applicants and adjusting Thoreau's recruitment processes and technology to better meet their needs, Virginia felt worlds better than she had back in January.

The inquirer pool had risen significantly over the previous year. What's more, several thousand inquirers had characteristics that looked strikingly similar to those of the previous years' stealth applicants. After they inquired, Virginia had sent special e-mail marketing messages to this group, inviting them to participate in newly added, online community forums and message boards. Many of them did just that. Virginia smiled, put down her coffee, and clacked out an e-mail to President Plutarch: "We've got a really good handle on the data, and I can confidently project record applications this year." She clicked "Send" and glanced downward at her unchewed fingernails "What can we do next?"

Chapter 11

Challenging Opportunity #2
What a Wicked Web

When first we practice to believe...

The EM Challenge

One warm July day, Dr. Benjamin Plutarch almost knocked over his morning coffee when he opened an e-mail message from Glynnis Johnson, a new trustee at Saint Constanza College. Dr. Plutarch had just recently become president of the suburban Philadelphia liberal arts school.

Johnson asked him whether he knew that an anonymous blog entry with an accompanying cell-phone video about a fraternity hazing incident at Constanza currently ranked in the Top Ten on Digg.com. "What incident?" he muttered to himself. "And what the hell is Digg.com?"

He decided to wait to respond to Johnson's e-mail message until he knew the facts, whatever they were. Plutarch, a scholar of medieval medicinal practices who had moved from Thoreau University to the smaller Saint Constanza in hopes of peaceful pre-retirement years, eventually found Digg.com and the reportedly offensive blog entry. How could you miss something titled, "Constanza Chaos: Chicks Crash Chi"? Plutarch opened the grainy video and then proceeded to knock over his hot coffee. What he observed Constanza students doing was simply not fit for HBO, let alone the Family Channel. Plutarch's expensive laptop computer shut down as hot coffee sloshed across the keyboard. The last thing he saw was that the blog and video had been opened by 3,600 people and rated by 412 viewers.

Thoughts of resignation briefly crossed his mind, but he dismissed them, determined not to let a changing higher education landscape and all that Internet stuff get the best of him. Wondering who else on the Board of Trustees knew about this potentially damaging situation, Plutarch had the presence of mind to summon the Dean of Student Life, the VP of Marketing, and the VP Enrollment Management to his office for an emergency meeting.

This scandalous item had been online for a week, apparently, and was now all over people's Facebook pages, too. With a sinking feeling, Plutarch sensed a rapidly spreading brushfire, an impression confirmed when Emily Hatchet, Saint Constanza's PR director, rushed in to say that a reporter from *The Philadelphia Inquirer* just called her for a comment on the video. The newspaper got the story from an editor at *The Saint Constanza Call*, the student newspaper. The *Inquirer's* new internship partnership with the *Call* had been proudly launched by the College only three weeks earlier.

The VP Enrollment Management reported that she had already received ten angry e-mails from parents about the incident. As bad as this is for any college, it was a particularly painful situation for Saint Constanza, steeped as was is in a deep faith tradition. Twelve admitted students had inexplicably withdrawn from the new freshman class in the last week alone. The loss of so many students so late in the cycle at such a small college was a very big deal.

Just when Plutarch thought things couldn't get worse, his executive assistant indicated that Marty Kodelski, one of Constanza's biggest alumni fundraisers, was on the phone. Plutarch reluctantly took the call. Kodelski and Glynnis Johnson were law partners; no doubt Glynnis had spilled the beans. "Ben," boomed the normally affable Kodelski, "I'm looking at this video and I really can't believe my eyes. We have that Million Dollar Club fundraiser next Tuesday and I can't be twisting those arms with this stuff floating around. What are you doing to fix it?" Kodelski hadn't received the video from Glynnis Johnson, but from a colleague of his in Tokyo who got it via e-mail from a friend. It seemed like President Plutarch was among the last to discover the dreadful video.

The C² Opportunities

Know The Facts

What happens on the Web doesn't necessarily stay on the Web, as Saint Constanza College soon discovered. Achieving an understanding of what key constituencies know and think about an emerging problem means taking a systematic approach. And this generally requires getting the facts straight. Of course, an institution will never get all the facts, and some of the "facts" it acquires will be wrong. Still, Saint Constanza's leaders need to know what happened and how it happened before they decide what to do and how to do it.

Saint Constanza's leadership was utterly lacking in real-time situational awareness, a condition the scholars call being "clueless." Dr. Plutarch should ultimately examine why they were in the dark and had to discover something like this from a trustee. However, as tempting as it is to play the "blame game" during a crisis, doing so can be enormously draining and counterproductive. The primary objective at this point is to understand the situation, understand how your constituents see it, and resolve it. This requires that someone on staff with a background in social networking media be added to the crisis team. Truly understanding a community these days means knowing it from both the physical and online perspectives.

Know Yourself

Achieving understanding requires a patient, respectful tone that allows employees to tell the higher-ups the truth. Schools can easily see an incident like Saint Constanza's mushroom into full-scale crisis, fueled in part by its own frenzied, defensive manner. When Sarah Martin, a recent Saint Constanza graduate working for the school's PR agency, Dodgem Nowe, was asked to join the ever-enlarging mob forming around the President's conference table, it would have been a good time to consider that the size and frenetic nature of the working group was itself communicating a crisis to anyone nearby. Not surprisingly, observers e-mailed their co-workers and neighbors to say, "Something big is happening. I just saw the lawyers and the PR people running into Plutarch's office."

Saint Constanza's leaders must consider that everything they do and say in such a situation conveys more about "the Saint Constanza experience" than any viewbook. After all, the true nature of a person's (or an institution's) character is often best revealed under duress. With its religious and spiritual values in mind, how Saint Constanza handles this crisis – with discipline, grace, and fairness – can actually move the school forward. How a school acquits itself in difficult situations can either inspire community members to represent the institution either well or poorly.

Know What You Don't Know

President Plutarch might have surmised that his own people – the school's students, alumni and friends – were using word-of-mouth and e-mail to present Saint Constanza in a very poor light. Marty Kodelski was already separating himself from the school with his money people, and the Agronomy Department down the hall was doing everything but sending smoke signals to communicate the crisis, whatever they perceived it to be. In the age of instantaneous communication, speed really does count.

When Sarah Martin asked President Plutarch how Constanza planned to respond, he barked: "We need a statement that says we'll launch an investigation, we don't condone these actions, we remain committed to the highest traditions of religious values, and we will take all appropriate disciplinary actions." When Martin asked whether Plutarch wanted to do his own YouTube video in reaction, his only response was "Huh?" Emily Hatchet added, "We need something. The *Inquirer* just called again." That's when Plutarch screamed, "It's a morning paper! We don't have to get back to them until later this afternoon!" Gently but firmly, Hatchet replied, "The print version means nothing. They want this on their website now and they're going to link it to Digg.com."

Conclusion

The Saint Constanza crew sat in silent dejection around the conference table in President Plutarch's office, until the Dean of Student Life broke the silence. "You know, we're a pretty small place in a pretty tight community. I've been here for five years now, and I don't recognize any of those students."

The Dean of Student Life was correct. The video had nothing to do with Saint Constanza. It was shot and uploaded to YouTube and then merchandised across the Internet by students at nearby Owens Landing College. It seems that after the Saint Constanza Capulets inflicted a humiliating football defeat over the Owens Landing Oligarchs, revenge seemed ever so sweet.

From the conference table, President Plutarch placed a call to Owens Landing President Betsy Hoople. After initially signaling disbelief and then bringing her lawyer onto the call, Hoople realized that the video's "cast members" were *her* students, not Saint Constanza's. Ultimately, she agreed to investigate the situation, discipline the students, and immediately prepare a letter acknowledging that Saint Constanza's students had nothing to do with the video. Saint Constanza requested and received approval to use the letter in all communication with its community, as needed.

At its next offsite meeting, the Saint Constanza leadership team reviewed the many lessons learned from the incident. Plutarch reminded everyone: "What you think you know can hurt you as much as what you don't know." In assembling their first-ever crisis response team, they also learned that it is easier to disrupt a community than it is to build one. Being impressed that Saint Constanza College cared enough to communicate the truth about the incident to them personally, seven of the 12 defecting admitted students chose to attend Saint Constanza after all.

Chapter 12

Challenging Opportunity #3
Seduction Most Rank

To be or not to be – you.

The EM Challenge

Dr. Candace Roberts, President of Chicago's "Loop"-based Oldham University, was about to make a presentation to her Board of Trustees about the *US News & World Report* rankings. One of her trustees, Jeanne Langton, was concerned about Oldham's rankings, having done an analysis showing that Oldham had been penalized for its large proportion of adjunct faculty. Indeed, President Roberts had done a calculation with her Executive Vice President, Murphy James, which showed that Oldham could jump ten notches in the *US News* National University rankings if it reduced the proportion of adjunct professors. A resultant higher ranking could dramatically increase national interest in Oldham and possibly lead to larger applicant pools.

And yet Roberts and James both knew that Oldham's distinctiveness and academic quality were related to its location in downtown

Chicago, where world-class practitioners, CEOs, famous actors and musicians were available to teach on a part-time basis. Only three years earlier, for example, the Music Department formed Outside the Musician's Head, a new performance curriculum developed and taught by leading singers, songwriters, musicians and producers. When OMH was announced, its new PR director at the time, Emily Hatchet, was quoted in the *Chicago Sun Times* as saying, "Families are investing so much in higher education today. They want to make sure that their students have access to the best practitioners in their fields. Oldham truly understands this point, for which we are forever grateful." Roberts loved the quote, since she felt it mirrored her own sentiments. Hatchet's previous experience in higher education certainly fueled her passion for the subject. She long felt that the college where she previously worked was insufficiently focused on what she called "real-world job skills."

Besides, what about Rocky Perish? Perish founded the megastar rock band, Perish the Thought, upon his Oldham graduation ten years ago. He was also a member of the OMH advisory board and a serious candidate for a major donation to the university. The students and adjunct faculty members just loved Rocky, which was apparent to anyone reading "Thinking about Perish the Thought," the cover story in the latest issue of the Oldham alumni magazine.

Roberts was reading a different newspaper article, about the embarrassing resignation of Owens Landing President Betsy Hoople, when James sat down to start their planning session for the coming Board of Trustees meeting. Trustee Langton had specifically asked that the *US News* ranking issues be placed on the agenda. When the day of the Board meeting arrived, the question was framed as, "What are the tradeoffs associated with decreasing the proportion of adjunct faculty?"

The C² Opportunities

Fulfilling Needs

Oldham had recently hired DataMeaning Associates to undertake market research on prospective students, current students and alumni. President Roberts just last week offered the opinion that, "Far too many schools are trying to engage students without knowing much about them." Besides, Roberts always liked DataMeaning President Ben Magruder who, as it turns out, was a very big fan of Rocky Perish, too.

 DataMeaning's research found a direct correlation between students' need for marketable outcomes, such as good jobs and higher salaries, and their confidence that faculty with real-world experience can help to achieve those outcomes. So, Roberts and her leadership team understood the level of engagement and inspiration students actually felt they received from adjunct faculty members.

Representing with Pride

 Research also found that to the extent that alumni feel Oldham has kept its promises and prepared them for real-world engagement, they are more likely to sing its praises – quite literally. Such passion by alumni can support the school in many ways, such as a desire on the part of graduates to recruit new students and to participate in alumni panels on career preparation and advancement. Indeed, the alumni who were surveyed enjoyed serving on these panels because it gave them a chance to collaborate with the faculty they loved and remembered so fondly. "All these constituents seem so interdependent," Roberts thought.

DataMeaning's survey of current students and alumni helped identify the factors that affect their satisfaction or dissatisfaction. It also gathered information on the ways in which alumni wish to remain connected to the university through services and programs. This is precisely why, after seeing this market research, the leadership team's goal became the development of institutional pride, both during and after the student experience.

Stewarding the Message

 Oldham was also adept at generating generally favorable publicity throughout Chicagoland and well beyond. They had used the market research to develop a highly differentiated brand strategy, market position and messaging system that addressed the specific needs, desires and concerns of their audiences. This reflects the fact that they took time to know their audiences and to massage the message in a way that resonated with them powerfully.

Oldham's messaging spoke to the special attractiveness of world-class practitioners on the faculty as well as the role of student experiential learning and a vigorous, well-connected career-education office. Leveraging the myriad experiences of their graduates, they were able to develop messages that inspired their target student demographics to apply and enroll. In doing so, they reinforced the idea that Oldham is not all things to all people, delivering a distinctive ap- proach to education that is nonetheless just right for some people.

Of course, President Roberts would not be satisfied until every member of her leadership team went through message training. "Long gone are the days when everyone is saying such different things about the place. We have to learn how to stay on message." She was impressed with Emily Hatchet's quotes in the Chicago media. Perhaps after three years working at OMH, the PR maven might be ready to return to a post in higher education.

Conclusion

President Roberts was well prepared for the Board meeting. She led a vigorous discussion that seemed to capture most of the trade-offs associated with adjunct faculty and the implications for the *US News* rankings. She had the ammunition she needed to offer a compelling alternative to any seductive quick fix. As she challenged the efficacy of "gaming" the rankings to gain immediate results, she made a strong case for preserving a precious asset, Oldham's adjunct faculty. After all, the answer was right in front of her all the time, in the form of the Oldham Mission Statement. It read, "To educate and train a collaborative community of students, faculty and alumni determined to contribute to the day-to-day practice of science, business and the arts." Roberts worried that without objective market research findings to support her, the Board seemed all too willing to veer away from this core mission. That's when she determined that Oldham ought to undertake this very research every three years, comparing results over time and adjusting to the changing demands and opinions of important constituencies. She told James, "This issue or something like it, will arise again, I'm sure. And we'll be prepared with information and insights when it does."

EM=C² ■ Chapter 12: Seduction Most Rank

Chapter 13

Challenging Opportunity #4
Underendowed Ambitions

To level the playing field, look to your values endowment not to the value of your endowment.

The EM Challenge

Phil DeCoffers, Senior Vice President for Marketing & Communications at West University in St. Louis, called an urgent meeting of the school's senior leadership team. In recent days, local media had been joined by several national outlets in their attentive coverage of President Rich Pockets' announcement of some rather lofty ambitions for the university – too lofty and ambitious, some on campus believed. President Pockets had begun to enjoy the spotlight a bit too much. Each additional news story seemed to compel him to make even more provocative claims about the impending ascension of West University above and beyond its more elite competition.

President Pockets had taken the notion of going out on a limb to new levels. It seemed to DeCoffers as if he and the other Senior Vice Presidents were being pulled onto that same fragile limb with him.

The President had recently committed West to constructing several new buildings, increasing admissions selectivity, recruiting additional highly regarded faculty, improving academic quality, and – here's where DeCoffers thinks he hears that limb beginning to creak under the weight of these promises – all the while increasing affordability and access. DeCoffers, steward of the institution's value proposition and careful shepherd of the institution's mission and message, realized it was time to get together with the other senior leaders to discuss delivering on all these promises. It would be a difficult conversation, since DeCoffers knew that doing the right thing for the institution was not always the right thing to do for his career. No matter what he said at the meeting, he believed that President Pockets' blind loyalists would cast him in an unfavorable light. "I can hear the whispering already," he said to his wife Kim. "They'll say, 'Phil's not on board with Rich's vision.' "

How can DeCoffers, the Senior VP for Advancement, Senior VP for Enrollment, Provost, and the CFO make all these promised improvements happen? "It doesn't seem possible," DeCoffers acknowledged after the last member of the group pulled a chair up to the conference room table. The CFO chimed in, "Where will we find the money? We're going to need to accelerate tuition increases and raise our goal for the capital campaign." West, founded 150 years ago by an order of monks who played a little known role in America's westward expansion, has over 5,000 undergraduates and several thousand more students seeking advanced degrees. The endowment stands at just over $200 million, so the school is not poor. Since 70 percent of the endowment consists of restricted funds, however, and the "reach" schools that Pockets would like to zoom past all have endowments well over $1 billion each, the puzzle appeared unsolvable.

The Provost complained, "You all know how expensive it is to recruit and hire new faculty at this level." The Enrollment VP added, "We are already 'gapping' most of our needy students, while at the same time 'buying' candidates at the top of our academic profile. More aggressive increases in tuition and fees will negatively affect our recruitment of a talented and diverse student body." The VP for Advancement objected, "Of course we need money, but our current goal for the campaign is already a stretch. Even if we had the prospects to justify an increase in the 'Go West, Young Scholar' capital campaign, it's not easy to find donors to fund our priorities. Major gift prospects want to give to what *they* care about."

Successful implementation of Pockets' vision – his "Promise" as he's been calling it – would require sustained and steep progress in various dimensions of the entering class profile and retention, significant revenue increases, and a dramatic shift in public perception, competitive positioning, and the university's value proposition. That said, West's direct competitors have far more money and, currently, greater perceived value and prestige. The team had only an hour to discuss the dilemma. (After that, DeCoffers and his wife were heading to a Rocky Perish and Perish the Thought concert.) He flashed a slightly self-pitying half-smile. "Many of our prescribed objectives appear mutually exclusive. And I doubt that any other universities are going to simply let us sprint by them *even if* we can solve this Rubik's cube. Heck, they've got enough endowment money to match our investments and *still* underprice us in terms of net tuition! Some of them have already announced they will reduce their effective tuition costs while improving the quality of their offerings." His mouth widened ironically. "So, any ideas?"

The C² Opportunities

Break the Walls

West University's senior leadership team knows there are intractable conflicts among the institution's important mission commitments, the objectives implied by the President's vision, and the practical realities of the university, its assets, and its position on the competitive landscape. This team would be the first to agree that the most worthy sets of challenges are often the most intimidating, and they genuinely admire the

President's ambition for the institution. They agree in principle that the best way to regain a sense of optimism is to look at the puzzle in a brand-new way. Maybe the dilemma isn't quite what it seems to be. One of the most difficult things to do in high-level decision-making and management is to think outside the box, because it's so rarely obvious that any of the talented and intelligent professionals involved is thinking *inside* the box in the first place. In this case, what if the box is the mere premise that there is conflict in the goals and that any solution will, by necessity, be some form of artful compromise? What if the box is the notion that the competition with more prestigious institutions has to be on *their* terms? What if the box is the idea that the leaders at West have to take on the assignment precisely as President Pockets imagines it? Maybe there are other methods that could support the achievement of all the goals, after all.

Reframe the Game

Before making any other moves, the team has an opportunity to consider the constituencies the university serves and hopes to serve, and that they must involve for any subsequent efforts to succeed. Prospective parents and students, current students, alumni, and past donors are just a few. Reaching out to ask these audiences about their opinions, desires, objectives, and values opens the door to extracting valuable information.

What if donors would welcome donating money for financial aid, but are lukewarm about giving money for another building? What if prospective parents and students are passionate about a particular part of their belief system that isn't currently served in similar ways by other universities? After all, the monks who originally built West were a devout, admirable group of men. What if current student satisfaction with West hinges on faculty interaction and the quality of their experience far more than the listed price of tuition or the non-academic amenities on the campus?

It's critically important to identify the starting point: *What do West's communities care about?* Without it, the university is playing on someone else's turf, accepting someone else's rules for a game that ought to be about this institution's own unique proposition, mission, and experience. At the outset, West can understand why students enroll, what makes them satisfied, and why alumni donate time and money. Understanding why individuals join or don't join these communities, how they experience these communities in fulfilling their needs, and why they might or might not represent and steward the institution feeds the possibilities for how to move forward.

Return Inward

When an institution like West University has aspirations to move in directions it has never traversed in the past, the most important thing to remember is to remain authentic. In this book, we say "embrace your genome," but all that means is make sure you understand who you are at the core and don't stray from that in simple pursuit of statistical metrics. If DeCoffers and the senior team find that some of the "what ifs" above are in fact the case, many avenues open up that allow West to thrive while maintaining its distinctive identity.

Consider the scenario where West identifies several arenas that are of powerful interest to their desired communities that are not being served by the aspirational competition. West can choose to compete on those grounds instead of competing on grounds already well-worn by the competition. There's no need to compete on the basis of who the competition is, but rather on who West University truly is and wants to be. Suddenly, the entire set of challenges takes on a completely different dimension, one that doesn't require West to convince the world that they are "better" than the big, wealthy competition. If West University is utterly unique, the need for direct comparison dissipates.

Redirect the Ship

It is from this frame of mind that DeCoffers and West University can begin to craft the message of inspiration to join, experience fulfillment, represent and steward the institution on its voyage. In this scenario,

West might decide, in appreciation of the desires of its students and alumni, to create an "Institute of Ethical Inquiry" that bridges faith and academia. The Provost could set an objective to recruit the very top professors in this field. DeCoffers could clack fiercely on his keyboard: "The premier values-focused institution in the Midwest, extending its impassioned commitment to faith and academic exploration, will break ground on the groundbreaking institute this coming Spring! This year, we raise our capital campaign goal not to support bricks and mortar, but books and mortarboards. West University's most ambitious campaign in its history seeks to build intellectual capital. This year, we recommit ourselves to our mission instead of a climbing wall; innovation and discovery instead of a new weight room; excellence we can be proud of instead of more flat screen televisions."

West could continue to raise tuition at a reasonable rate while the VP for Advancement makes financial aid the annual fund's focus in the coming year. With rising enthusiasm, DeCoffers hits his laptop again and frantically pounds out the crux of another winner: "West University's commitment to academic opportunity and affordability is unmatched. This year, all of our annual fund donations will be directed to provide financial support and grants to reduce the cost of education for enrolling students. Our goal is to raise enough money so that every student admitted to West University can afford to attend and receive the world-class education, rooted in faith, which the University has offered since its inception."

Realize the Goals

Now, there's no telling that it will always work out smoothly or that West University's efforts will magically achieve a set of difficult objectives, but let's consider what might happen if the pieces fell into the places we've envisioned above. Through understanding, inspiring, engaging, and leveraging, what might be the outcome for West University in light of President Rich Pockets' exuberant declarations?

If West offers opportunities for the desired communities to engage the university by connecting to issues for which they have great passion, the unique and mission-based capital campaign may, in fact, successfully create a prestigious and notable new Institute. In turn, this lures high-quality faculty members, which in turn improves the quality of academic offerings, all of which support the recruitment of a talented student body. Annual fundraising for financial aid, which has been anecdotally viewed as a successful fundraising approach in the current educational climate, may support the grants and scholarships required to enroll elite students. Such students may be drawn away from more selective competitors in part by the uniquely appealing message regarding the new Institute, new faculty, and enhanced academic offerings, in addition to the financial support and incentives.

Conclusion

In what might seem like a highly unlikely twist, President Pockets and West University just may end up with what they sought. It may not transpire quite as the President might have imagined, by ramping up direct competition with more elite competition, but by recommitting to a creative and aggressive expression of the most authentic and intimate version of West's true mission. Instead of playing on the wealthier institutions' turf, West chose to build on its own deeply held values.

DeCoffers and his colleagues convened one of their routine "tracking" meetings, as they had been doing regularly since that worrisome first session. By all reports, they were beginning to realize that the school really has produced the best possible expression of a compelling value proposition. It was the best way to break open the box and let the excitement and enthusiasm for West University pour out. DeCoffers had just started speaking when President Pockets strode confidently into the conference room and said, "You know, not too many leadership teams collaborate and cooperate as you do. I knew you would figure this out, and I'm proud of you. Now, let me tell you about my plans for the first-ever West Medical School."

Chapter 14

Challenging Opportunity #5
Global Poaching

Secure your inspirational – not your geographical – borders.

The EM Challenge

It's early July - well after Staple University's May 1 deposit deadline for the fall class. While many colleges and universities breathe a sigh of relief and anticipate a successful close to a busy year's enrollment cycle, the enrollment picture at SU is tempered. As an urban comprehensive university located in Hartford, the university enjoyed steady enrollment growth for its first 85 years. Much of this growth came from outside New England, as the university pursued building a more national and international student body.

As the quality of the university's applicant pool has increased, however, so too has the quality and prestige of SU's institutional competition. In fact, recent trends indicate that SU is increasingly competing for what were once its bread-and-butter students against not just other domestic institutions, but institutions outside the United States. In recent years, SU and other schools have seen rising numbers of prospective students choosing to apply to and attend colleges in Canada, Europe and Asia.

Susan Smith, Director of Enrollment, and Thomas Vine, Associate Director of Enrollment, have spent much of this sunny Friday afternoon poring over application and enrollment statistics, trying to understand the implications. Susan must attend an Executive Committee meeting on Monday morning and present a summary of Staple University's enrollment picture. Turning toward Susan, Tom asks if this is a trend or a fluke, and what new initiatives should be undertaken to respond to the immediate and possibly longer-term problem. He recalled a helpful presentation at the last meeting of the National Association for College Admission Counseling (NACAC) in which the speaker, Virginia Rhodes from Thoreau University, addressed this issue of "global poaching." She told the audience that her institution was also wrestling with the issue of "stealth applications," but added that so many of the global and technology factors had combined in recent years to make the enrollment management job exceedingly difficult.

He also recalls Rhodes hinting over coffee at NACAC that she was unhappy at Thoreau U and looking for another job. "Oh, that's right," Susan replied. "She was working for Dr. Plutarch, but he left there to take that Saint Constanza job. I remember reading something about him online."

"OK, where are those notes?" Tom muttered out loud. "Here they are! Let's see what Rhodes suggests."

The C² Opportunities

Understand the Motivation to Join
Staple University needs to understand what motivates its prospective students (inquirers and admitted students). They should develop a very specific, empirical

sense – beyond opinions about what they *think* they know – of what prospective students are looking for in a college experience and how this compares to what Staple offers. The school should attempt to understand the relationships that exist between students' likelihood of applying to and enrolling at SU and their demographic characteristics, educational priorities, and assessment of SU and its primary competitors.

 Susan must be sure to survey not only those who applied and enrolled but also the "dark matter" populations of those who Staple lost – the non-applicants and non-matriculants. Their perspectives are essential to learning the most influential factors in students' decisions. This feedback will reveal which impressions of SU affected students' application and enrollment decisions, and whether primary influencers were academic, financial, social, location preferences, or some combination of these factors

In the research, students should be asked to identify the schools to which they are considering applying or have already applied. Staple should pay special attention when analyzing the results to identifying the priorities and opinions of prospective students who are considering non-US schools. Specifically, Staple should learn how students find and gather information about non-US institutions, what draws them to consider enrollment at these schools, and which of these schools is considered best and why.

Experience the Search

The research with prospective and admitted students should be designed to understand the experiential nature of the college search process. Rhodes told the NACAC audience they should try to understand and even "feel," in emotional terms, the user friendliness of the application process, timeliness of the financial aid award, quality of information received after acceptance, programs offered after acceptance (Open Houses, Admitted Student Receptions), and overall quality of interaction with the Admissions and Financial Aid Offices.

 Through the research with prospective students, the University will learn what messages resonate best with key audiences, especially students inclined to international learning, and how they can serve as a foundation for a strong messaging platform. Staple will also understand how students learn about the school and what are the best vehicles for delivering a coherent set of messages across print, digital, electronic and interpersonal media. Susan smiled cynically at that point in Tom's review of his notes, observing, "We can't get this place to focus on any consistent messages for more than two weeks!"

Represent Your Interests

 Routinely analyze the competition, making sure this includes the University's non-US competitors. Assign the gathering and assessment of "competitive intelligence" to an extremely capable Admissions staff member. The analysis of data and recruitment material for comparative purposes will enable the university to better understand the market in which it competes.

SU needs detailed knowledge of the marketing practices and messaging platforms of its overlap and aspirant competitors, in order to represent itself well. Positioning the university in relation to its competition, both domestic and international, can be an extraordinary challenge. After all, an institution is being asked through the brand-development process to move away from jargon and cliché and explain in meaningful terms why it is really different and truly matters. This is the essence of creating the brand promise. By investing time in this essential work, best-practice schools are able to identify that singular piece of their heart, mind or soul that becomes a powerful, attractive manifestation of their true selves. They become better equipped to represent themselves to prospective students and others while also fueling the willingness and ability of key constituents to represent the school with pride and passion. Tom's notes reflect these sentiments well. "It's the 'eureka' moment that most schools never find."

One way to get there is to conduct a "Stealth Inquirer Exercise" in which a hypothetical student inquires as a prospective student both to SU and a selected set of competitors, including top international competitors. The timing of first response and follow-up communications, the content, and the visual appeal of the communications will be examined and compared in order to better understand SU's positioning, distinctiveness, and the competitors' key messages.

Leverage the Globe

Another way to tackle the problem head-on is to make sure that core recruitment messages include information about successful alumni. Prospective students are frequently drawn to individual profiles and blogs of current students on university websites. Institutions ought to engage successful alumni to participate in much the same way.

For SU, ensuring that brochures and online materials include numerous profiles of alums (especially those who have found fulfilling lives and careers overseas thanks to the innumerable benefits of an SU education and diploma) is just another step in spreading their distinctive message that students need not be educated at international colleges to find success abroad. The power of good stories allows prospective students to connect and engage with the potential that SU provides, even if that potential may take them away from the United States after graduation, that an institution on the other side of the world might not. Simply put, remind them that SU can fulfill their global dreams

without sacrificing all the benefits of an American education.

When Archimedes said: "Give me a place to stand and a lever long enough, and I will move the Earth," he may not have been thinking about leveraging the world in quite this way, but a college or university can give its alumni considerable leverage by providing them with a strong academic experience upon which

to stand and proclaim the value of that experience to the world.

To Steward or Not to Steward

How familiar are students with their domestic and global alternatives? What is the relationship between cost and value in their minds? When they matriculate

at a given school, here or abroad, how do they evaluate that experience? Do they remain at the school as satisfied students or, in the case of those attending overseas institutions, realize after their first year that they just want to go home? Can they find a "home" at your institution, and what will that take to build and sustain? Answering these questions correctly will reveal a continuum that takes prospects from curious applicants to successful students to satisfied graduates and then to passionate stewards. Each link in the chain requires

authenticity and fortification at the time of the experience, but the final result of doing so is the development of a cadre of brand stewards who become the living embodiment of any institution's brand promise.

Conclusion

Susan and Tom had what they needed. At minimum, Virginia Rhodes' guidance at NACAC gave them the inspiration for managing this situation very well. Furthermore, the insights they were developing would ensure that Susan had the right set of arguments and recommendations for Monday's Executive Committee meeting. Still, she understood the dangers. She knew beyond any doubt that building and sustaining a vibrant, multidimensional Staple University community required unprecedented teamwork among the executive staff.

"Understanding, inspiring, engaging and leveraging community members is deeply discounted, if not entirely lost, by continuing to work in such rigid departmental silos. That's not how the world sees us, although it is how we are organized," she said. Tom agreed, "The world is way too complex these days to make these artificial separations between students and alumni. We have to take a systems approach to building and nurturing community." "That's right," Susan replied, "the moment a student enters this place he or she should be treated like a prospective alum. And the moment a student becomes an alumnus, we should be inviting him back here for more learning – and even some teaching. Students are alums and alums are students across a never-ending enrollment continuum of joining, fulfilling, representing and stewarding. Everything's changing, and it's pretty darn exciting."

That's when Tom added, "Hey, I see from Virginia's notes that day at NACAC that there's a new book and website on this very subject; it's a new kind of enrollment management called EM=C²."

Chapter 15

To the Energized Go the Communities

Like the original notion of Enrollment Management, EM=C²
requires energetic leadership and a robust organizational
commitment.

The title of this chapter harks back to Jack Maguire's seminal article, "To the Organized Go the Students."[34] Now, over 30 years later, we propose broadening the discipline of Enrollment Management beyond students to embrace all manner of interconnected communities. And yet, the need for an energetic philosophy of collaborative implementation remains as essential today as it has ever been.

The problem, as anyone knows who has labored for long within the walls of academia, is that a college or university can't simply be instructed to "change." An institution is, after all, a C^2 entity – a Community of Communities. In such an organizational environment, change is a complex dynamic that needs to be understood, respected and undertaken with great sensitivity – not commanded from the podium or manipulated behind the scenes. Real change, in other words, can only be infused, not imposed.

The Leader as Energy Distributor

The effective institutional leader seeking change, therefore, must recognize that in a Community of Communities his/her task is to nurture connections within and among these communities and facilitate win-win moments of understanding that help bring about change. In effect, such a leader empowers others through the distribution of leadership energy.

This is the kind of distributed leadership that Margaret Wheatley speaks of in her highly acclaimed book, *Leadership and the New Science*.[35] According to Wheatley, the Newtonian leader operates in a hierarchical, reductionist mode, disaggregating large tasks into their component parts and then delegating responsibility for each part to subordinates. The "new science" leader, Wheatley argues, adopts an approach more evocative of holograms, chaos theory and genetic biology by articulating a core formula that defines the set of distinctive values and behavioral norms of the enterprise. Then the leader seeds that formula throughout the organization, empowering everyone to lead in their respective areas in accordance with those central tenets. The result is a self-replicating, self-reinforcing infusion of values throughout the institution and beyond. The President, as the key player initiating and reinforcing this process, must embody this philosophy and promulgate it throughout the institution.

Will New Presidents Be Prepared?

With a large-scale turnover in college presidents anticipated over the next 5-10 years,[36] more new presidents will be confronting this increasingly daunting world of Enrollment Management. Will they be prepared? Our 2005 Presidents Survey revealed considerable room for improvement in presidential preparation even then.

41% of respondents indicated that they felt "very well prepared" for their first presidential jobs.

46% felt they were "moderately well prepared" and **10%** "slightly well prepared."

Silo, Can You Go?

Even the most inspirational and energetic leader, however, can use some practical tools to help break down those isolating silos and put in their place the enclaves of collaboration that are so essential to the cultivation and leveraging of communities. We would point to the following mechanisms as being particularly useful:

- ## Adhocracies

  This term, popularized by Alvin Toffler [37] in the 1970s and further developed by Henry Mintzberg,[38] refers to the use of temporary, *ad hoc* groups to address particular issues or take on tasks requiring the concerted effort of dedicated teams drawn from different parts of the organization. Unlike its polar opposite, bureaucracy, the adhocracy is able to function without regard to formal structures and reporting relationships. *Ad hoc* task groups focusing on institution-wide issues of Enrollment Management defined in C^2 terms, for example, would enable a broader perspective to take hold even as the various functional departments are retained. A whole new cadre of administrative staff (and faculty) can be sensitized through actual collaborative, *ad hoc* work experience to the value of this broader perspective and be counted on to carry this way of thinking back to their respective departments.

- ## Integrated Systems

  As we noted in Chapter 6, advances in information technology now make it possible to track all of the transactions (or touch points) between school and individual prospect, student, alumnus, donor, parent, etc. throughout their lifetimes. Thus, it is far more feasible than ever before to manage a process that involves the simultaneous cultivation and maintenance of multiple communities populated by these same individuals. As successive generations of these IT systems have become increasingly integrated across the institution, they have also become the common ground upon which all of the previously isolated organizational units must operate or cease to be effective. The integrated systems enforce a kind of awareness and appreciation of the transactions occurring elsewhere in the organization with regard to the same populations – or, as we would put it, the same communities.

- **Dashboards, Templates and Common Metrics**
  Sometimes getting people on the same information system, in the same room, or even in the same virtual space (synchronously via conference call or webinar or asynchronously via e-mail or wiki) is not nearly as effective for instilling a sense of shared purpose as is getting them on the same page. By this we mean getting them to agree to use a common reporting format – such as a so-called dashboard report – that highlights a set of cross-functional or institution-wide performance indicators.[39] Selected properly, these common metrics require a collaborative mindset to yield positive results. Combined with meaningful incentives that include liberal doses of recognition and celebration of jointly achieved goals, the "same page" can soon become the same C^2 enterprise.

- **New Silo-Spanning Positions**
  The emergence of a host of novel organizational positions and titles is one of the more intriguing contributions of the software design and dotcom worlds. Many of these titles, like Chief Person Officer, Money Master, Chief Imagination Officer, and the like are intended to reduce workplace formality and boost employee enthusiasm. Some titles, like Chief Evangelist, better reflect how user communities are actually cultivated in cyberspace than do more traditional titles like Marketing and Promotions Director. We see in this trend an opportunity for colleges and universities to borrow a page from the businesses that thrive in the e-commerce "space" by creating positions that both reflect the realities of a networked marketplace and, by definition, span the traditional silos. Directors and VPs of Student Engagement, for example, are popping up on campuses these days in an attempt to provide a point of management focus for a "retention"

function that has long fallen between the cracks of the several departments that serve student needs, from academic counseling to the registrar and bursar's offices. Perhaps there is room in this mix for a Chief Community Cultivator, whose role might be to facilitate conversations about particular communities across the Enrollment / Retention / Alumni Affairs / Advancement divides.

Wanted: One Parallel Universe (Wormholes Included)

Even with all of the above systems and organizational possibilities, the question remains: Is it, in fact, possible to transform an entire institution into one that functions from a C^2 perspective? Can this expansive, multi-dimensional way of thinking and doing coexist in parallel with the more traditional, Newtonian approach to Enrollment Management with its sequential funnel phases and preoccupation with the battle for student yield?

We must admit that introducing a C^2 sensibility to the practice of Enrollment Management may for a time require a process of structured experimentation and parallel processing. We can envision EM=C^2 as a parallel universe but with a few built-in "wormholes"[40] that permit transformative energy to pass from this new universe into the old.

A good illustration of how this might work can be found in institutions that are developing regional strategies. We are aware of at least one major university that has established a regional working group (an *ad hoc* task force comprising members drawn from across the university) with a very clear charge to maximize the leveraging potential among an array of communities within a particular geographic region. The group is being asked to identify – and where possible to quantify – these communities' interests in relation to the university as well as their prospects for building student enrollment, providing financial support, and their synergistic potential. Among the communities under consideration are: trustees, alumni, current students, parents, college counselors, student-identified influencers (teachers, other role models), foundations, knowledge experts, former faculty, and internship-sponsoring employers.

Even as the rest of this university continues to function as it always has, this working group is experimenting with the C^2 model. They have been granted permission to go off and do some serious playing in a regional sandbox and, to the extent that they succeed in their efforts, have been asked to share what they have learned with the rest of the institution. Other regional initiatives based on what has been found to work will undoubtedly follow. Will the university as a whole adopt this new paradigm? Well, we suppose only spacetime will tell.

———

Our conceptual sights may roam far beyond our own universe of universities, but the everyday realities of institutional life and the internal as well as external competitive pressures shaping those realities require that we take an unsparing look at the organizational infrastructure within which we would hope to pursue a C^2 model of Enrollment Management. Many a bold voyage has foundered on the shoals of short-sighted self-interest. In our view, the silo culture so endemic to the world of higher education represents the single most threatening obstacle in the path of realizing the potential of this new formula for Enrollment Management. It was the biggest obstacle to be overcome three decades ago when EM was first envisioned, and it remains so today.

What is desperately needed is energetic leadership committed to re-capturing the C^2 – Community of Communities – spirit of the educational enterprise.

Our CommenC=EMent Address

*To honor your persistence through our EM=C² curriculum it's only fitting that we deliver a commencement address. So here it is: **www.thecommunitysquare.com** Let the dialogue commence!*

We have tried to make the case that the current system in which EM is practiced isn't dealing very well with today's challenges and opportunities. College and university presidents, trustees, and other leaders are contending with a rankings-fueled set of marketplace forces that encourages them to persist in an outmoded, ineffectual way of thinking, lest they lose some kind of tactical advantage. The only way to transcend this paralyzing dilemma is to adopt a whole new view of what Enrollment Management as a professional discipline is all about.

We conclude (and commence) with some big thoughts about how to deal with this brave new world. Here are a few we've put forward in this book:

- **It is not about control.**
  It's way too late for that. Communities that have an impact on your institution, whether for good or ill, are forming all the time;

you can't stop this physical and digital reality. You can only acknowledge, understand and thoughtfully influence the process. Go into it and learn – and teach – from the inside.

- **Embrace your genome.**
  Know who you are, what you stand for, and what you want. Then seek out your allies, your supporters, your communities. And, guess what – it's also the way out of Rankingdom. Which is not a bad thing.

- **You gotta love IT.**
  Today, Information Technology in cyberspace and on the campus is the experience of community. Don't fight it. Harness it and use it to better Understand, Inspire, Engage, and Leverage communities.

- **Recognize that your institution is a C^2 entity – a Community of Communities.**
  That is your strength. You don't stand apart from your communities—present, past, and future. All those communities are you. You are they! So you are entitled to weigh in and seek to shape – not control – them, but always, always in keeping with your distinctive DNA of mission and values.

Meet You Online in The Community Square!

Now it is time for colleges and universities to do what they do best – teach and learn. As Jack likes to say: "When I started as Dean of Admissions, I didn't know anything. Fortunately, I was able to convince people that it was in everybody's best interest to teach me what they knew."

And so, we hope this book encourages institutional leaders to teach not only their colleagues (and us) but also business and other enterprises what it means to attract and sustain communities of scholars, students, donors, and a host of constituents over time; expand the boundaries of knowledge, and perpetuate institutional legacies from one generation to the next. We also hope this book will challenge these same leaders to learn from the worlds of business, cultural anthropology, social networking, information technology, and other fields; and apply what they learn to the special, community-driven realities of the academy and campus.

In keeping with the premise of this book, let us take advantage of today's technologies to teach one another. We now invite you to learn with us, as you share your own experiences and insights. Our goal is to "do" what we want to "be" – namely, employ the very technologies that are changing the institutions we serve in creating our own Community of Communities (C^2). Toward that end, we've set up a website where the conversation can begin:

http://www.thecommunitysquare.com

You will find in this online version of *The Community Square*, conversational threads that we began to weave in Chapters 6-9. You will also find discussions there informed by the foundational articles, research and case studies that we draw upon for many of the concepts in this book.

But that's just to prime the pump. We're eager to let the ensuing conversations go wherever they will. We ask you to weigh in with examples of how you may already be applying C^2 principles even without referring to them as such. In the end, we will answer together how Enrollment Management can most effectively meet the many challenges facing institutions of higher education today.

Adopting a new formula for Enrollment Management – **EM=C²** – with Community at its core is a good place to start.

Notes

1. These are composite cases based on real experiences with clients, but with the names and other details changed to protect the innocent.

2. Maguire, true to his professional training as a theoretical physicist, was quick to discern how quickly the mathematics of organizational complexity can escalate. With just these four departmental silos (Admissions, Financial Aid, Registrar, and Student Information Systems and Research), a single EM Director would need to manage as many as 10 organizational interactions – the 4 departments plus the 6 bilateral interactions between those departments [in accordance with the formula: $N=(n-1)/2$].

3. John Maguire, "To the organized, go the students." *Bridge* Magazine, Boston College, 1976: 16-20.

4. The emergence of "Strategic Enrollment Management" (SEM) is one such expansion of the concept which, in our view, is inherently redundant inasmuch as the original concept was itself grounded in a strategic perspective.

5. On our dedicated website: www.thecommunitysquare.com we provide a continuously updated listing of some of the more influential EM thought leaders and their writings.

6. To date, in no institutions that we know of, have the offices of fundraising, alumni services, and development been integrated under the expanded purview of Enrollment Management, despite their originally having been conceptualized as participants in a life-cycle understanding of enrollment management extending into the alumni years.

7. Including: *The Princeton Review, Washington Monthly, Kiplinger,* Vanguard Scholars in the United States, and Times Higher Education - QS World University Rankings, Shanghai Jiao Tong University's *Academic Ranking of World Universities*, and *Newsweek's* ranking of The Top 100 Global Universities.

8. Such as National Survey of Student Engagement (NSSE), Cooperative Institutional Research Program (CIRP), College Board – SAT, Admissions Testing Program (ATP), and ACT.

9. In an effort to combat the influence of the *US News* rankings, many schools have begun to turn to the National Survey of Student Engagement (NSSE) as their best hope for reframing the national dialogue on quality. Citing NSSE's research about the positive impacts of "student engagement" on enrollment statistics and outcomes, *USA Today* has developed an online information portal for institutions willing to participate and share their NSSE data. Based on self-reported student behaviors, they provide some insight and beneficial institutional research (complementing a rankings system), but in our view, they don't offer the level of concrete measurement it would take to divert attention from the powerhouse that *US News* has become.

10. Here's what *US News* says: "Certainly, the college experience consists of a host of intangibles that cannot be reduced to mere numbers. But for families, the *US News* rankings provide an excellent starting point because they offer the opportunity to judge the relative quality of institutions based on widely accepted indicators of excellence. You can compare different schools' numbers at a glance, and looking at unfamiliar schools that are ranked near schools you know can be a good way to broaden your search. Of course, many factors other than those we measure will figure in your decision, including the feel of campus life, activities, sports, academic offerings, location, cost, and availability of financial aid. But if you combine the information in this book with college visits, interviews, and your own intuition, our rankings can be a powerful tool in your quest for college." (Robert J. Morse and Samuel Flanigan, USNews.com August 17, 2007.)

11. As noted in "Who is Managing Your Institutional Image – Your Institution or *U.S. News & World Report*?" Presentation by Kathleen Dawley at The College Board's Colloquium 2000, January 23-24, 2000.

12. Although SAT scores officially account for less than 10 percent of the overall ranking score, a study by Thomas Webster determined that the average SAT score for enrolled students is far and away the greatest factor in determining institutional rank. Webster found that the correlation between SAT average and ranking was 0.89 (with the highest average SAT scores associated with the highest ranked schools.) Kuh and Pascarella, "What Does Institutional Selectivity Tell Us About Institutional Quality?" *Change* Magazine, September/October 2004.

13. As reported in "The Net or the Noose: Develop sustainable financial aid strategies to prevent budgetary troubles," by Linda Cox Maguire, in *University Business*, January 2007.

14. An "SAT Optional" movement has been gaining ground in recent years as one way of escaping this double bind. Unfortunately, in all too many cases, schools that adopt this policy continue to re-

port average SAT scores for ranking purposes that are inherently skewed higher because those that elect not to submit their scores tend on average to score lower, leaving the pool more heavily populated with higher scores. Another concern is that disproportionately represented among those admitted without having submitted SAT scores are students with greater financial capacity to pay full tuition. To the extent this is the case, SAT Optional works against increasing socio-economic diversity. Thus, we see that SAT Optional, rather than serve as a truly high-minded rebuke to the rankings, can become yet another self-serving way to game the system or achieve other institutional goals.

15. As noted above, there are now several annual publications that rank global institutions, not merely those in American higher education. A May 2007 *Chronicle of Higher Education* article reported: "When a small group of researchers at Shanghai Jiao Tong University, in China, started comparing the world's top research universities, their aim was to help China develop world-class institutions of its own. But their annual "Academic Rankings of World Universities," first published in 2003, quickly became a popular international reference. The ranking is based almost entirely on measures of strength in research. It looks at such indicators as the number of faculty members whose papers are highly cited, and the number of faculty members and alumni who win Nobel Prizes. The result is a list of what Shanghai Jiao Tong says are the world's 500 best institutions. In 2004 *The Times Higher Education Supplement*, a British weekly, introduced its annual *World University Rankings*, which list 200 institutions. Those rankings are based half on the opinions of faculty members and company recruiters, and half on the ratio of full-time academic staff members to students and on how often faculty members' papers are cited. Although the ranking has not achieved the influence of its Chinese competitor, the two lists have had considerable impact in just a few years, especially outside the United States." Bollag, Burton. "College Rankings Catch on Overseas." *The Chronicle of Higher Education*, May 25, 2007.

16. In 2007, one organization took a strong public stand against the rankings and even persuaded quite a few college presidents to sign a letter pledging not to participate in them. Despite their pledge, however, it appears that a number of these institutions continue to promote their rankings on their websites and in their marketing materials.

17. Comparing the 2008 *US News* ranking of Top National Universities with the 2007 NACUBO ranking of colleges and universities by market value of endowment assets, we find that the top 20 *US News* institutions are all listed among the 20 most highly endowed private institutions with the exception of Johns Hopkins (tied for 14th in the *US News* ranking and 21st in endowment value), Brown (tied for 14th in the *US News* ranking and 22nd in endowment value), and California Institute of Technology (tied for 5th in the US News ranking and 28th in endowment value). Even within the 20 top-ranked schools there is a remarkable correspondence between endowment size and rank order. The top 4 schools have the top 4 endowments; those in the middle of the pack tend to have endowments valued in the middle range of the top 20; and those near the bottom of this elite set of schools, according to *US News,* have endowments similarly clustered on the NACUBO list. The same overall congruency of endowment value and *US News* rankings holds up on a per-student basis, once you account for a few small, richly endowed institutions like Rockefeller University.

18. According to The College Board's 2007 *Trends in Pricing* report, national averages for published tuition and fees have increased (for private institutions, public institutions, and even two-year community colleges) continuously for the past 25 years, even after adjusting for inflation. Especially for private institutions, the same is true even for net price, after financial aid grants are taken into account.

19. Responding to Congressional and competitive marketplace pressure, between December 2007 and March 2008, two dozen highly selective institutions eliminated loans from their financial

aid packages or reduced tuition directly for some or all of their students. Primarily targeting lower and middle income families, these institutions made it more affordable for the select few students in these income brackets that are qualified enough to be admitted. In all, 18 of the 24 institutions have endowments of $1 billion or greater. It is indeed a case of wealthy institutions providing a valuable service to families while deploying their resources to even greater competitive advantage over those without billions.

20. The *Chronicle of Higher Education* in April 2008 reported that "the proportion of financially needy undergraduates at the nation's wealthiest colleges and universities actually dropped between the 2004-5 and 2006-7 academic years. Just 13.1 percent, on average, of the undergraduates at the country's 75 wealthiest private colleges in 2006-7 received Pell Grants, which are awarded to students from families with annual incomes of less than $40,000. Two years earlier, Pell Grant recipients made up 14.3 percent of the student body at these colleges, which have endowments of $500-million or more. "Wealthy Colleges Show Drop in Enrollments of Needy Students," by Karin Fischer, in *The Chronicle of Higher Education*, April 24, 2008.

21. Some might argue that the graduation decision is also one that is made by the institution, inasmuch as it is the school that certifies through the granting of a degree that the student has satisfactorily fulfilled the course requirements. True, the institution establishes a set of academic requirements and other regulations, but it's the student's choice whether or not he/she follows those rules and completes the work. If in fact the student does so, the institution certainly does not have a choice whether or not to authorize the student to graduate. If the conditions are met by the student, conferring the degree is a matter of process, not choice. In other words, it is a proactive set of actions by the student that leads, or does not lead, to a degree. In our view, assigning the decision to the institution at this funnel stage would unnecessarily diminish

the considerable agency residing with the student – who, after all, is the "paying customer" in this model.

22. Shirky, Clay. *Here Comes Everybody: The Power of Organizing Without Organizations*. The Penguin Press, New York, 2008.

23. McMillan, D.W. and Chavis, D.M. "Sense of Community: A Definition and Theory," *Journal of Community Psychology*, Volume 14, January 1986, 6-23.

24. *ibid.* p. 11. (Note: We modified slightly some of the words in parentheses for the sake of clarity.)

25. Butler, Lawrence. "The M-SAT: Maguire Strategic Aptitude Test" Presentation in the Maguire Associates Resource Room archives at: www.maguireassoc.com/resource/index/html

26. To learn more about these technologies, recent trends in their use in higher education, vendors and their integrated, administrative applications, see:

    a. Harris, Zastrocky and Lowendahl. "Magic Quadrant for Higher Education Administrative Suites, 2007," Gartner, Inc., September 26, 2007.

    b. Finnegan, Webb and Morris. "2007 NACAC White Paper. Technology in the College Admission Process: Impact on Process, Professionals and Institutions," National Association for College Admission Counseling, 2007.

    c. "IT on the Campuses: What the Future Holds," *The Chronicle of Higher Education – Information Technology*, April 4, 2008.

    d. EDUCAUSE: Transforming Education Through Information Technology (www.educause.edu) An excellent online resource for current and historical papers and research studies on the use of IT in higher education.

27. Sara Corbett, "Can the Cell Phone Help End Global Poverty?" *The New York Times Magazine,* April 13, 2008.

28. Jack Maguire and his colleagues have long made it a point to informally "interview" waiters, waitresses, cab drivers, and folks from all walks of life about what school they attended and how their educational experience has affected their lives. This has proven to be a tremendous reservoir of qualitative research.

29. Charlene Li, "Trends – Social Technographics®: Mapping Participation in Activities Forms the Foundation of a Social Strategy," Forrester Research, April 19, 2007.

30. Sometimes referred to in the nonprofit sector as Constituency Relationship Management, CRM for our purposes might be more appropriately termed Community Relationship Management.

31. In summarizing the findings of Maguire Associates' research, *The Chronicle of Higher Education* stated: "Ask college faculty members about the high-school graduates coming into their classes: Many will tell you that students are ill prepared for the demands of higher education. Ask public high school teachers the same question: While they acknowledge student shortcomings, their answers will be more positive." Alvin B. Sanoff, "What Professors and Teachers Think: A Perception Gap Over Students' Preparation," *The Chronicle of Higher Education*, March 10, 2006.

32. There is some evidence from our *Chronicle* survey data, however, that alumni assistance has been less in demand, as some enrollment staff have come to rely more on high-tech rather than high-touch modalities.

33. In case you are having difficulty interpreting the symbolism of these icons, they are: UNDERSTAND = Magnifying Glass; INSPIRE = Flame; ENGAGE = Hand (Touch); LEVERAGE = Lever; JOIN = Key; FULFILL = Diploma; REPRESENT = Pennant; STEWARD = Column Capital (Support).

34. We referred in Chapter 1 to this 1976 article in Boston College's *Bridge* Magazine, noting that the title was not the author's

preferred choice, as it might be misconstrued to call for "organization" in a structural sense. Even then, the key driver of EM was not some organizational fix but the spirit and energy behind a proactive, data-driven effort to break down the silo mentality that kept critical functions from collaborating.

35. Wheatley, Margaret J., *Leadership and the New Science: Discovering Order in a Chaotic World*. Berrett-Koehler Publishers, San Francisco, 1999.

36. According to a 2007 article in *USA Today* reporting on a survey of 3,396 presidents conducted in 2006 by the American Council on Education (ACE): "College presidents have gotten older and have been in their positions longer than at any time in the past 20 years, indicating an upcoming wave of turnover at the top.... Nearly half of the 2,148 leaders of public and private institutions who responded to the ACE survey were at least 60 years old. Only 14 percent of presidents were over 60 when ACE first surveyed presidents in 1986. Also, presidents reported being in their jobs an average of 8.5 years, the highest recorded average since the survey was first conducted." Groppe, Maureen, "Report: 'Major turnover' of college presidents on way," *USA Today*, February 12, 2007.

37. Toffler, Alvin, *Future Shock*, Random House, New York, 1970.

38. Mintzberg, Henry, *Mintzberg on Management*, Free Press, New York, 1989.

39. For more information on the design and implementation of "dashboard" reports, see: Butler, Lawrence, *The Nonprofit Dashboard: A Tool for Tracking Progress*, BoardSource, Washington, DC, 2007.

40. According to Wikipedia, "A wormhole is a hypothetical topological feature of spacetime that is basically a 'shortcut' through space and time" – sort of like a worm taking a shortcut to the other side of an apple by tunneling through its center.

Acknowledgments

In an effort to model the community sensibility we've espoused in this book, we have tried to make the writing of it a truly collaborative project within our firm. Employing an array of techniques from online wiki and collaboration platforms to bi-weekly book discussion sessions, we developed our thoughts together with our colleagues. In the end (or rather in the middle of what we hope will be an ongoing process), this endeavor has paid off in ways we could hardly have imagined at the start. The biggest payoff has been the appreciation we've gained for the hard work of harvesting collective insights and hammering out boundary-stretching ideas – and, no less importantly, for having a lot of fun along the way.

So, we're very much indebted to our Maguire Associates colleagues for the good spirit with which they took on the challenge of thinking deeply and creatively about the larger possibilities of Enrollment

Management, even as they continued to cope with the pressing needs of clients. We would like to express particular appreciation to the following members of our team who, with great enthusiasm, undertook particular tasks.

Kathleen Dawley, Linda Cox Maguire, Tara Scholder, Sarah Parrott, and Jessica McWade threw themselves into the "Five Challenging Opportunities," animating what might have been a dry case-writing exercise into an entertaining set of stories. Jessica was especially helpful in giving these stories a common feel and light-hearted tone.

Andrew Thacher was a true partner in conceptualizing the EM=C² model, contributing any number of key ideas along the way. He and Jessica brought us important understanding of the technologies and organizational disciplines upon which this new EM paradigm is built.

Jonathan Epstein, our game utility infielder, who, despite a heavy commitment to completing his masters degree at Harvard, contributed significantly to several chapters (especially, Chapter 1: Original Synergies and Chapter 2: Rankingdom Rules).

Apart from their always insightful suggestions, Leslie Horst and Rob Mirabile were tremendously helpful in drawing from our *Chronicle* surveys more compelling findings and quotations than we were able to accommodate in this book.

We also want to thank Patricia Casey, Mark Maguire, David Wuinee, Roland Stark, Haley Rosenfeld, and Jonathan Copp for their valuable inputs; and the other members of the Maguire team: Trina and Sujoy Das, JoAnn Presti Daskalakis, Johanna Janka, and Qin Lin for their participation and encouragement. And, of course, we are always grateful to Anne Heller, Kristine O'Neil, Todd Graf and Paul Brady for keeping us all well-organized, well-fed, and generally in an up-beat state of mind throughout this intense effort.

On the production end, we want to thank Kate Victory (a name that proved prescient) for her wonderful editorial touch. She was a sure-footed guide and boon companion through the sometimes treacherous pre-publishing terrain. Thanks also to Ken Lizotte at emerson consulting group for his wise counsel and good instincts in assigning Kate to work with us. Special thanks to Patty Brady, graphic designer extraordinaire, for her technical skill and good humor in turning mere typescript into a real book. Thanks also to Missy Scott for her invaluable assistance with the index.

We cannot close these acknowledgments without thanking the most important community of all – our clients. Over 400 of them, as we enter our 25th year as a firm. If C^2 means anything, it means that we are part of a "community of communities" constantly learning from and teaching one another. We thank our colleagues and clients for being the best teachers we could ever have.

EM=C^2 ■ Acknowledgments

Index

ISBN 142516875-2

Edwards Brothers Malloy
Oxnard, CA USA
November 26, 2014